MW01632296

JUSTICE FOR SLOANE (POLICE AND FIRE: OPERATION ALPHA)

SAN ANTONIO FIRST RESPONDERS BOOK 1

REINA TORRES

CONTENTS

Dear Readers,

Welcome to the Police and Fire: Operation Alpha Fan-Fiction world!

If you are new to this amazing world, in a nutshell the author wrote a story using one or more of my characters in it. Sometimes that character has a major role in the story, and other times they are only mentioned briefly. This is perfectly legal and allowable because they are going through Aces Press to publish the story.

This book is entirely the work of the author who wrote it. While I might have assisted with brainstorming and other ideas about which of my characters to use, I didn't have any part in the process or writing or editing the story.

I'm proud and excited that so many authors loved my characters enough that they wanted to write them into their own story. Thank you for supporting them, and me!

READ ON!

Xoxo

Susan Stoker

Susan Stoker – you have my thanks and lots of aloha for your friendship and your encouragement. Your heroes and heroines are always an inspiration and I hope that I've done your world justice.
Mahalo-

ACKNOWLEDGMENTS

Thanks to Thuy Phan for her staunch support and sharp eyes. You were a huge help!

And to Miriam Rivera and her lovely mother, Sanjuanita, for their lovely assist when my Spanish language skills came up wanting.

CHAPTER 1

Walking into the San Antonio FBI Field Office, Special Agent Vicente Bravo stared at the nearly empty room. Director Jack Travis walked into the room and stopped short. "What are you doing back, Bravo?" Taking a step to the side, he looked at his calendar. "You still have a few days of your vacation left."

Vicente let out a sigh. "I was tired of the beach."

"Tired," the man's voice was rough with disbelief, "of the beach."

He didn't know why he'd said the words. It was stupid, but it was close enough to the truth.

"The noise. My parents six of us. Their parents had a lot of children. And I… well, I can handle them a few at a time, but having them all together for a family reunion sounds great."

Holding his hands up in surrender, the Director shook his head. "No need to elaborate. I only have two and they produce enough noise on their own, but I worry about inner ear injury when their friends are over at the house."

Vicente tried to hide the instinctive grimace at the

thought of a bunch of teenagers that close to him for hours on end. "So, it was easier to tell my family that you needed me back in the office."

"Well that works just fine for me, Bravo."

Maybe it was the way the director said his name with more than a hint of eager anticipation, or maybe it was the gleaming look in his eye, but either way, Vicente was starting to wonder why he didn't just stay at the beach, grab a drink and find an umbrella with his name on it for a nice long nap.

"What do you need?"

Again, stupid question, but he'd asked it.

"Come into my office."

Vicente followed the director and by habit closed the door behind him. He watched as the computer started up and brought up a browser and then continued on to YouTube.

"Only the finest in surveillance for the FBI, Boss?"

That earned him a pointed look. "Want to be the 'Keeper of the Copier Room,' Bravo?"

"No, sir."

Leaning over his desk, Director Travis started typing in keywords with his pointer fingers.

On a different day, Vicente could have ribbed his boss over the ineffective typing method, but he was already in enough warm water. There was no need to jump into the boiling pot beside it.

"When I find the video, I'll show you why the office is pretty much a ghost town at the moment but suffice to say that you literally walked in at the perfect moment.

"You've been tracking down fugitives for the last few months, pulling in some great numbers, but I need you to shift to a side branch of the Human Trafficking Task Force for a little bit."

"What kind of *side branch* are you referring to, sir?"

"Something popped up today and I was coming back to the office to see who I could pull in for a special assignment," he gave him a big smile. "You'll be working in connection with the task force, but not in the thick of things, so you won't have to catch up with anything. What do you know about Sloane King?"

Vincente felt like someone had shifted gears in their conversation. "Sloane King?"

Director Travis nodded.

Ticking off the salient points of what he knew took just a few seconds. "Texas Royalty. Old Money. Socialite. Philanthropist. If there's a ball or a fundraiser where the wealthy and the glamorous are expected, she'll be there."

He saw the director digest the information and a smile curled his lips.

That couldn't be good.

It was *never* good.

"I was asked to find a guard for Sloane. For the next few days at the very least. We have some indication that she may have been targeted in some way by the traffickers and we've been asked to assure her safety."

Vicente was sure he was suffering from a delayed reaction to heat stroke. That had to be it. He was delusional. Hearing voices.

And yet, there was his director smiling at him as if he knew exactly what was going on in his head.

No.

Not this Special Agent.

"You want me to spend my next few days doing what?" He gave his boss a look that spoke volumes. A whole encyclopedia. "You want me to babysit a Texas Beauty Queen?"

Director Travis leaned against his desk, keeping his eyes trained on Vicente's face. "She's gorgeous, but as far as I know she doesn't hold any titles." A stranger might have thought the director guilty of some deadpan humor, but he was serious about the titles.

After spending the better part of the last decade in the San Antonio Field Office he knew enough about the director not to challenge him on pageant knowledge. Both Addison Travis and Mary Louise Travis had held the title of Little Miss San Antonio and Miss San Antonio. Their mother Joan had made it all the way to Miss Texas before she married Jack. It was only a matter of time before the girls followed in their mother's high-heeled footsteps.

"Maybe I should have said debutante, but you know what I'm saying. Sloane King is a paragon in San Antonio, not to mention someone constantly in the public eye. Who would try to hurt her?"

Leaning forward in his chair, the director reached for his mouse and clicked on the video he'd queued up.

Vicente moved closer to the desk and leaned on the edge to watch.

The dark screen flared white and then settled onto an image. After a strange stuttering of the image the video began to move. After a moment, the image was altered, tightened down by a frame that splashed a headline on the screen.

TERRIFYING HIGHWAY CHASE

A local news station's emergency cut in coverage of the high-speed chase from that morning, leading out of San Antonio. The minivan that the police had been following for miles had already crashed into an embankment when the video cut to the footage and the site was littered with emergency personnel and vehicles.

It wasn't hard to find Sloane in the crowd. Her long sable-colored hair was pulled back into a ponytail and she was in the center of a group of women and a few police officers.

Even with all the rank pins and chevrons decorating over

a score of first responders and law enforcement in the area, Sloane looked like she was in control of the situation.

What galled him was that no one seemed to find that the least bit odd. A young officer standing just off her shoulder was staring at her with an expression that could be construed as more than a hint of idol worship.

Or worse, bold-faced desire.

Rookie.

The footage continued with the overly enthusiastic voice over from the 'on-the-scene' reporter and Vicente felt a pinch of irritation between his shoulder blades.

"...before the first ambulance left the scene, homegrown Texas philanthropist, Sloane King, was onsite organizing help for the victims of what appears to be another sex-trafficking abduction thwarted by law enforcement. What the hell-"

The already frenetic scene erupted into chaos as gunfire split the air.

The young police officer at Sloane's shoulder jerked back and began to drop as another volley split the air and Sloane grabbed at her upper arm.

The rest of the footage played out before him in slow motion even though the image on the screen continued to play in real time. Sloane should have run like everyone else looking for cover or dropped down to the ground and hidden under anything she could find to try to avoid another hit. Instead, she lowered the officer to the concrete and covered him with her body. Police officers on scene returned fire and closed in around their compatriot, making a shield with their bodies. They had bullet-proof vests.

Director Travis clicked the PAUSE button and then left the mouse alone on the desk and cleared his throat.

"Before you even think of trying to pass this off, don't. It's your fault for coming back early from your vacation and walking in right after I had my ass handed to me." He stretched his neck and tugged at his collar. "I just had a call from both the Mayor and the Governor's offices. They have *suggested* in the strongest terms that the Task Force extends protection to Miss King."

"Protection from?"

"Whoever shot at her today."

"What indication do you have that she was the target? How many other people were injured by the gunfire?"

"Three," Director Travis grudgingly admitted. "Besides the police officer, one of the EMTs took a bullet to the leg, and one of the suspects took a bullet to the gut."

"It could be as simple as that. Trying to silence one of the suspects before we could interrogate them." Vicente looked back at the screen at the wall of police officers still visible in the final shot of the video. "There hasn't been time for an investigation to know the exact target."

Director Travis gave him a single nod in answer.

"Who's in charge of that? I'd rather be out there looking for the shooter. I'm not one for babysitting socialites."

There was a pause before the director spoke again. "We've known each other long enough that I'm going to take that as you having *a moment* and not as an unhealthy dose of insubordination." Sitting up close to his desk, he set his forearms on the edge. "I want you on this, Bravo. That's all there is to it."

The Director nodded and turned away toward his computer. "You'll meet up with her at the hospital. Agents Fry and Porter are there at the moment. They'll join in on the investigation once you're there."

The 'moment' Director Travis was speaking about may have gone on longer, but whatever sense of preservation left in Vicente, his love for his job, turned him around on his heel and moved him toward the door.

He'd keep the princess safe, but if his boss thought he could be called off the search for the shooter, then working together as long as they had, hadn't taught Jack Travis much about him. Not by a long shot.

❧

Sloane King laid her head back against the wall and let the world tumble by. The Emergency Floor at Feldspar Hospital was still teeming with people a few hours after the shooting.

It wasn't the first time she'd been to the Emergency Room in the course of her work. She'd seen and helped women after all kinds of terrifying and tragic moments in their lives.

Held hands.

Soothed crying children.

Helped family make final arrangements for their loved ones.

But this was the first time that she was the one getting medical treatment from an injury received during her work. Helping women and children navigate the scariest moments of their lives wasn't just her vocation, it was a labor of love.

Shifting on the bench, she winced. The bandage that was put in place at the scene of the accident hadn't been changed yet, but she'd insisted that the women recovered in that morning's raid were seen first.

It should have been the natural progression of things, but she'd recognized one of her uncle's people in the ER, trying to move her to the front of the line.

Even after she'd tried to explain that she was happy to wait her turn given the triage priorities they'd received in the field, the staff had been nervous. She didn't blame them. Glen McKinnon, her father's closest friend and their almost 'uncle,' could get a dog to meow if he set his mind to it, but she'd assured the staff that as the head of the Hopeful Hearts Foundation that was footing the bill for the women brought in during the raid, she was more than capable of and willing to wait her turn.

Maybe it was just her imagination, but over the last few minutes the din had finally begun to quiet as the police were joined by FBI in clearing the press from inside the hospital.

She had no idea what time it was, her phone had been lost in the shuffle when gunfire had split the already noisy scene into frightened fragments of the crowd it had been.

Just a short while ago she'd sat beside the wounded officer's mother, holding her hand as the doctor came out to give her the prognosis. The bullet had done its damage to his shoulder, but he would survive. It was going to be a long road ahead and mother and son were all the family they had.

Sloane made sure that his mother had a hotel room near to the hospital for the night and dinner delivered to her from a local restaurant. It was the least she could do for a woman who'd had a close call with losing her son.

She'd lost family over and over again and remembered how lonely and alone it made her feel. She didn't want that for anyone else.

Not when she could do something about it.

Now, alone in the hallway, Sloane was struggling to fight off the nagging pain in her arm. If someone didn't call her in to see a doctor soon, she was likely to fall asleep right there.

She wasn't big on needles, and cold linoleum floors gave her the creeps, so if she could avoid it, that would be great.

"Hey, lady."

She didn't have to look to know who it was at the end of the hallway. Hildie Faraday, her sorority sister and best friend, was approaching. The rapid click of her Jimmy Choos was unmistakable in the echo of the hallway.

"I've got an update for you."

Sloane knew it was good news. Hildie's voice was better than a lie detector. She couldn't hide her feelings. It was one of the things that had kind of bonded the two in school. Hildie spoke her mind and Sloane kept everything bundled up inside.

"How are things going?" Sloane tried to open her eyes. She got them to flutter open a bit but gave up a moment later and kept her head right where it was. "Do you need me to come and help?"

A soft touch to her shoulder said that Hildie was right there beside her. "We're good. The girls all had superficial injuries from the crash, but we made follow-up appointments for them to check for additional issues that might pop up. The girls were starved so we called Patty and she sent over more than enough food for them while we contacted their families."

Something squeezed tightly around her heart and worry reared its head. "How did that go?"

A light kiss on her forehead came with a soft laugh. "Careful, you'll prune up with worry lines."

"Hildie-"

"Goodness! Patience, woman! It went just fine, Sloane. One of the girls has family in Nacogdoches so they're leaving tonight to come and see her. The other girls are in a hotel room and they have security from the San Antonio Police Department."

Sloane tried to nod, but just ended up with a soft groan instead. "And the Foundation-"

"We're paying for the food, the rooms, and we're taking them to one of the Helping Hearts and Hangers locations tomorrow to get them some clothes."

Sloane felt a grateful smile stretching across her lips and sighed like she'd just had the last bite of caramel and custard goodness of her favorite flan. "Thanks, Hildie. You're a godsend."

"I'm just so happy you're okay, sweetie! I couldn't believe it when Rolando called me this morning. You could have-"

"Miss King?"

Oh wow. As far as voices went, she had a thing for deep and thick. Well, other things too, but voices that fit that description? Yes.

"Are you Sloane King?" Whoever he was, he had a voice like chocolate sauce, warm and delicious.

"Oh, wow, you have to look at him, Sloane. Goodness!"

By the breathy tone of Hildie's voice, Sloane imagined her old friend fanning herself and fluttering her eyelashes.

Prying her eyes open and lifting her head, Sloane looked in the direction of that amazing voice and concluded that she must be suffering from shock. Or on the other end of the spectrum, she could just be delusional because this man... whoever 'he' was, was gorgeous.

He wasn't overly tall, but he was built. Even with his utterly basic suit she could see how the fit of the garment told her all she needed to know. He was strong, lithe, and muscled in so many perfect ways. He wore the suit, rather than the other way around, and made it look like Armani with his bearing alone.

"Miss?" His tone had taken on a quizzical tightness that almost sounded like worry. "*Estas bien*? Are you okay?"

She wanted to answer that she was fine, but at the moment her eyes were focused on his mouth. The warm cast of his complexion, mixed with the narrow set of his lips, even the close trimmed mustache and partial beard that framed his mouth had her thinking something completely out of character for a first meeting.

I wonder... she almost smiled... *if he kisses closed mouth or open?*

"I'm sorry, sir." She managed to sit a little straighter like her teacher had instructed her in her charm school class. "I've had a really crazy morning. I'm not at my best." She gestured toward Hildie. "If you need something, Hildie should be able to help you."

It shouldn't matter to her how excited Hildie seemed to hear that declaration.

But it did.

And it shouldn't have meant anything when he shook his head and turned back to look at her.

But it did.

"I came here for you, Miss King."

Oh wow.

All kinds of long-dormant nerve endings flared to life and even as she sat there in the cool air-conditioning of the hospital hallway, she felt like she was starting to burn.

"Well, that's something you don't hear every day." Sloane started to move forward on the chair to stand, and Hildie was there at her side, holding onto her good arm.

"You should sit, Sweetie. Your color's a little off."

Sloane brushed off her concern but used Hildie's hand to stand rather than stay on the chair. "I'm just in a bit of pain. As soon as they get to me, give me a new bandage, and hopefully a painkiller, I'll be right as rain."

He stepped up beside her and parted the halves of her sleeve to examine her arm before she could stop him. "You're still waiting to be seen?"

She nodded, looking away from the bandage. "It's been a zoo around here. I'm sure they'll get around to me."

The words she heard mumbled under his breath made her blush, but the way he gently set her back on the chair, carefully avoiding her arm, made her feel a warm tingle wherever he touched her.

"Stay right here."

He strode away and went straight to one of the nurses at the hub, catching her attention and holding it easily. Sloane smiled at the way the nurse's cheeks pinked. She didn't blame her, the man had a presence and confidence rolled off him like heat off the concrete in the Texas summer.

Nodding, the nurse turned and found Sloane's eyes as she hurried over in her direction with her dark-suited mystery man close behind.

"Sorry, Miss King," the nurse's voice was a little breathy, "we'll get you seen right away. Why don't you come with me?" The nurse helped Sloane into a private examination room. "Just sit right here and I'll have one of the doctors see you right away."

"Thank you," she looked at the nurse's name tag, "Amy. That's very sweet of you."

The nurse slid a glance and looked at the handsome man standing just inside the door. "Sure, anything for you, Miss King. I'll be on duty for another hour, so if you need anything," she managed to drag her gaze back to Sloane, "just ask for me."

Sloane swallowed her laughter and a little bit of something bitter off the back of her tongue. "Thanks again."

The nurse left, and on her heels, a doctor entered the room. He was tall, lean, and had a handsome smile on his face.

"Well look at this turn of events, Miss King."

Sloane rolled her eyes. "Doctor Clarke. What's with the grin on your face? Didn't your mama tell you that an injured woman isn't something to laugh about?"

"My apologies." He chuckled and looked at the clipboard in his hand. "But I beg to differ. My mama would indeed have my head if I was laughing, but I'm merely thanking my lucky stars that I'm the one that caught your case. I've been trying to get you to stop for more than a few minutes and maybe-"

Hildie made a little sound in her throat that sounded like a strangled squeal.

"Have a chance to ask you to dinner sometime."

"You were brought in here to look at her arm."

Sloane and Doctor Clarke turned to look at the man standing just inside the doorway.

Straightening, Doctor Clarke gave the man a stare as he folded his arms over his chest. "And who exactly are you to tell me my job?"

Reaching into his suitcoat, he pulled out a black ID folder and opened it. "FBI."

CHAPTER 2

Doctor Clarke visibly paled. "FBI?"

Vicente didn't know why it made him happy, but it did. "I'm here to protect Miss King."

That turned Sloane's head. She hadn't flinched when he identified himself as FBI, but the second part? It obviously didn't sit well with the injured woman.

Sloane blew out a breath that spoke volumes, but it was her friend's reaction that amused him. She looked him over head to toe.

And back again.

And nodded, slowly up and down with a smirk on her face.

"Stop undressing him with your eyes, Hildie."

He couldn't help but see Sloane's furtive glance in his direction before she gave her friend a pointed stare.

Hildie gave a vague gesture of shock and then leaned in to whisper in an overly-loud tone. "What about my hands? Can I use my hands?"

Doctor Clarke had apparently pulled himself together enough to speak up. "If you two would like to find a room together," he gave Vicente a smug look, "I can get back to examining, Miss King."

"I'm not leaving her."

Folding her hands over her chest, Hildie leaned her hip on the counter in the exam room. "This is good. This is really good. If I didn't think Sloane would disown me, I'd film this and put it on YouTube."

Sloane was stuck in place as the doctor cut off her bandage, but Vicente didn't miss the amused smirk on her face. Her friend may have no evidence of a public filter, but she was entertaining, and she made her friend smile.

Doctor Clarke laid the old bandage on the rolling tray that the nurse had set by the bed. Putting a hand on her elbow he lifted her arm into the light. "You should have called me. I would have come down and looked at you earlier."

"Everyone was busy."

"And she was busy taking care of everyone else." Hildie's indulgent sigh almost made Vicente smile. She didn't pull her punches.

"I can call a plastic surgeon in for you," Doctor Clarke turned her arm in a slightly different direction, "there are several that I can recommend."

Vicente watched as the man's words settled on Sloane. She craned her neck to look at the wound, but Vicente could tell that the movement was uncomfortable. Closing the door behind him, he moved to the other side of the room and picked up a mirror from the counter. He held it up for Sloane, so she could see the narrow crease along the outside of her arm.

Looking up at him, he could see the slight frown on her lips. "What do you think?"

The doctor bristled beside him. "You're asking him what to do? He's not a doctor."

And then it was Sloane's turn to take issue with the situation. "I'm getting a second opinion." She turned her head to look back at Vincente and seemed even more interested in his opinion. "Agent…"

"Vicente Bravo. I work out of the San Antonio Field Office." He looked over her wound and saw the torn flesh of her arm where a bullet had scored her in the attack. "Cleaned and stitched one way or another, as long as you keep it clean and avoid infection, I don't see why you'd need a plastic surgeon."

He could see the Doctor glaring at him over Sloane's shoulder, but Vicente didn't care one bit. He liked the look in Sloane's eyes. There was a kind of determination in them that he didn't see often.

And that he always respected.

Sloane shrugged one shoulder. "I might scar."

Vicente narrowed his eyes at her. "You worry about that much?"

"No." The answer was honest and immediate and was completely devoid of vanity. Interesting.

"Sloane," Doctor Clarke's tone was cold, cutting, "I'll have to insist that your guests leave so we can treat your wound. This is wasting my time."

Something happened. He could see the change in her expression and the warning in her eyes as she looked up at the doctor.

Looking down at her arm, he saw the pale outline of the doctor's fingertips. "You'll want to ease your grip on her arm, or I'll remove *you* from the room."

The doctor didn't take kindly to the interruption.

"You have no business talking to my patient about her care. I am the best trauma doctor in this hospital. Honestly, I was relieved that I was busy earlier when the mob came in, but as soon as I heard that Sloane was here, I came right down." He gave the agent a smile like he was posing for a headshot to go up on the wall in the hospital lobby. "After all, the Clarkes go back generations with the Kings.

"I just saw your uncle at the Country Club last Sunday when I was playing a round with the District Attorney and he said-"

"*He* meaning Sloane's uncle, or the District Attorney?"

They all turned to look at Hildie who just shrugged. "Sorry, I was getting confused by the name-dropping. I'll remain quiet while my friend continues to bleed."

❧

Sloane had just about had enough.

Doctor Clarke's complexion had turned a shade of tomato-water that didn't look good on the man. Then again, men like Doctor Clarke didn't like it when they stopped being the center of attention.

"I am sorry," Sloane began, "I know this is all very frustrating, but I don't want to keep you here if you were on your way out."

The doctor looked from her face to that of the agent, still standing less than a few feet away, and then back at her. "I'm sure your uncle would appreciate my assistance in your care."

Ah. There it was. He wanted to be remembered to Uncle Glen. While she wouldn't mind letting the man pad his ego and his markers for favors in the future, she didn't want to be subjected to his over bearing behavior. "Well, I'll make you a deal."

The doctor and the agent narrowed their eyes at her. Hildie was busy chewing on the corner of her bottom lip and enjoying the show.

"You can tell my uncle that you were instrumental in repairing my wound and I won't tell him any different."

The doctor's momentary smile faded a moment later. "And what do I need to do?"

Smiling, because she really was looking forward to it, Sloane told him. "Just get someone to come over and stitch me up. Any resident with a steady hand will do."

There was a moment, just a moment, when she thought he would take offense, but the promise to let him ingratiate himself with her uncle was just too good to lose. "Sure. Fine by me."

The FBI Agent pulled the door open and held it.

Doctor Clarke rolled off a glove with a snap as he stepped past the agent. It was almost comical to see the doctor push his shoulders back and stretch just the tiniest bit so that he was just as tall as the agent when he walked out the door.

Hildie sighed and waved at the empty doorway. "Bye now." That done, she darted forward and stepped into the doorway, holding out a hand to stop the door since the agent had let it go.

Hildie half-turned to speak as she kept her eyes outside the room.

"Oh, you should see the way he's walking down the hall. If he was any more of a dog he'd have a tail tucked between his legs."

"Don't say that." Sloane's voice was a soft plea. She enjoyed a good joke as much as anyone, but she also didn't want the agent to think she was mean. "I like dogs."

She couldn't help but notice the slightest smile on his lips.

"Good to know."

He wasn't sure exactly what to think about Sloane King. He'd expected her pageant-pretty smile to fade outside of the spotlight, but she was funny with her friend and sweet to any of the hospital staff that she'd come in contact with. With the exception of Dr. Name-dropper Clarke. Sloane had seemed like she was barely tolerating him.

Once her friend had given up on the running commentary of the stuck-up physician, Sloane had turned her attention to him.

He didn't bother trying to straighten his suitcoat or fiddle with his tie. He'd gone beyond that years ago. Still, people liked to judge him. The color of his skin. The origin of 'his people'. And with people of wealth like the Kings, they judged him on the price of his suit.

What he got when Sloane King finally focused her full attention on him was a cautious examination. "Hmm."

He looked back at her as his jaw started to tighten. "Hmm?"

She turned her gaze back down to her arm and let out a loud breath. "Let me guess," she touched a finger to the raw edge of the wound and swore under her breath, "Who called demanding that I have a protection detail? Mayor? Or, Governor?"

He felt an itch on the back of his neck. "Both."

"Ha!" Her friend standing beside the door pumped a fist into the air. "Called it!"

Picking up the purse on the chair, she reached in and pulled out a wallet.

Sloane looked at her in wide-eyed disbelief. "I could have gotten it out of my own purse, thank you."

Her friend shrugged and took out a twenty-dollar bill and folded it before dropping the wallet back into the purse. "But you just touched blood with your bare hands, so no thanks to the germs. Yuck."

With a triumphant smile she placed the folded bill down the neckline of her blouse.

Sloane grimaced and shook her head as she gave her friend a mock frown. "And bra money is better?"

A shrug answered her. "Why not?"

Sloane turned her gaze back to him and this time she skewered him with a look. "What do you say, Agent? If Hildie were to pull a twenty from her bra and hand it to you, would that be okay, or would you demand that it be disinfected?"

Well, this wasn't exactly what he'd expected from a first meeting.

He saw Sloane's expectant look and he had no doubt that her friend was also looking at him, waiting for an answer.

"After the events of this morning, Director Jack Travis of the San Antonio FBI Field Office has assigned me to guard you until the incident has been fully investigated and it has been determined that you are not in any danger."

He let the statement fall into silence and he waited for her to react.

All she did was turned to her friend, nodding over and over in little, barely-perceptible motions.

"Yep," Hildie nodded in response.

Sloane swung her gaze back up to him. "Nicely played."

He shook his head. "It's a statement of fact, Miss King. You were the apparent target of a shooting and we would be remiss in our duties-"

"Why the FBI, I wonder."

Her voice had a soft wistful quality to it, and distracting as it was he actually had an answer.

"The vehicles that attempted to intercept the van was part of our Human Trafficking Task Force."

She nodded, seeming to take the information in stride.

"The girls told me as much. A few of them didn't even realize they were inside the border. They'd been transported back and forth so much they didn't know where they were." Looking up at Hildie, Sloane opened her mouth to speak, but her friend beat her to the punch.

"We have our attorneys and social work staff meeting with the girls and immigration in the morning."

Vicente didn't notice that he'd tensed up until Sloane touched his arm and stroked her fingers a few inches along his coat sleeve.

"The girls will be given a chance, Agent. They weren't here on their own. As part of the task force, I'm sure you've seen a lot of inhuman and inhumane behavior.

"If the girls have family here and would like to stay, we'll make every effort to get them a Visa. However, if they would like to return home, we can also assist and give them a way home where they will be safe. These girls are all victims."

He nodded. "A lot of people forget that."

Sloane looked as if she was about to say something, but her lips remained closed.

Hildie stepped up beside Sloane and draped and arm over her friend's shoulders. "Sloane knows it more than anyone, Agent. You don't have to worry if we're on the scene."

He lowered his eyes as Sloane swiped her palm over each eye on turn.

"The FBI can offer you a stay at an area hotel while you're under our protection and-"

"We can use my apartment, Agent."

He hesitated, and her friend jumped in.

"She has a great security system. The whole complex has security cameras, and except for the random 'high class' call girls that go up to Four B, everyone in the building are good folks." She paused and then started again. "And be careful you don't get on Mrs. Carter's bad side."

She looked at Sloane who supplied the answer. "Two A."

"Yes, Two A. She's a one-woman Neighborhood Watch program." With a long sigh, Hildie shook her head. "She dinged me for loitering in the hallway with that attorney in Two C."

Sloane couldn't seem to stop the way the corner of her mouth curled up. "Well, she did you a favor, trust me."

A knock at the door drew their attention. A young resident in scrubs stepped in. "Miss King, I'm Winnie Cahill. I'm going to take care of your wound, so you can go home quickly."

Hildie arched a brow. "You trying to get rid of us?"

"No, Miss. But if you stay here any longer they're likely to put you in a room overnight and while the food here is improving, no one is a fan of the kitchen."

Laughing, Sloane held her arm out. "Then let's get stitching."

As the resident cleaned Sloane's wound and began the process of closing the wound, Vicente stood against the wall watching.

Contrary to the warnings from Dr. Clarke, not only was Winnie capable, she was pleasant and easy to be around.

In no time at all Sloane's arm was patched up and she was ready to leave.

"Hey," Hildie leaned in to her friend and almost-whispered, "you want me to go with you? For extra *protection*."

Sloane narrowed her eyes at her friend. "You got a black belt while I wasn't looking?"

Hildie looked shell-shocked. "Bite your tongue. Black isn't my color." The women shared a laugh. "No, silly, so you can protect the Agent from your neighbor. She'd snap him up in a heartbeat. He's hot, in case you didn't notice. So, keep a hand on him at all times or you'll lose him before you get inside your place."

Sloane kissed her friend on the cheek. "Go home, sleep, you've earned it."

Hildie returned the gesture and walked up to him, standing nose to his neck. "You keep her safe, or I'll make you pay."

He gave her a solemn nod. "She'll be safe."

Turning on her heel, Hildie moved for the door. "Well, I sure told him."

Alone for the first time, Sloane looked over at him. "I'm sorry, I'm about one minute away from falling asleep for a week. I know you told me your name, but…."

He took out his badge and set it in her hand, open. "Vicente Bravo."

She examined the badge before she closed it and handed it back. "Well, Agent Bravo," she smiled, "what naughty thing did you do to get babysitting duty?"

He saw her shoulders shake with laughter and her pearly white teeth peek out beneath her upper lip, but it was when she turned her full gaze on his, showed him the mossy green of her irises as she gazed up at him, that Vicente realized he was in deep trouble.

CHAPTER 3

By the time they'd left the hospital it was long past dinner, but Sloane didn't want to go in anywhere and sit down. She doubted that she'd make it through the meal without falling asleep in her food. Besides, she knew that Agent Bravo was going to have to tell her how this whole protection thing was going to work, and she doubted that he'd do that at a restaurant with lots of windows.

She heard him clear his throat and she looked over at him in the driver's seat.

He made sure he had her attention before he spoke. "I was thinking of driving through somewhere on the way to your apartment. Get something to eat."

"Sure."

A little bit of uncomfortable silence fell between them.

"Is there something you'd like? A certain place you'd like to go?"

She shook her head and then sighed. "No. I don't usually drive through-"

"Well, I don't think either of us is up to sitting in a nice place with tablecloths and finger bowls, and I'm sure that the places you usually eat don't do take out." She heard his soft cough of laughter. "Then again if I told them Sloane King was hungry, they'd probably send a chef to your house."

They slowed to a stop at a red light and Sloane turned toward him. It took a moment before he turned to look at her.

"I'm beginning to think you don't like me very much, Agent Bravo."

She watched the slight lift and fall of his Adam's apple, back lit by a twenty-four-hour laundromat across the street.

"I don't know you well enough to say that I don't like you," he qualified. "And really, it wouldn't matter if I did or didn't like you. I'll do my duty and protect you."

"You're right on the first part. You don't know me well enough, but you certainly don't like me. That's pretty clear." She sighed and turned back to look through the windshield. This was going to be a long night. "Could you pull over somewhere so we can talk, please?"

He didn't give her a verbal answer, but when the light turned green, the agent pulled through the intersection and turned into the parking lot of an orthodontist's office and came to an easy stop.

She sank back against the seat. She should have left well enough alone. Men didn't usually react well to the truth when they think it doesn't make them look good. Doctor Clarke was a good enough example. She'd have to wait and see if the agent fell into the same category.

But she thought that maybe the chip on his shoulder wasn't the same as the doctor's.

"Okay, I'm going to make a guess and if I'm wrong, then you should just go ahead and tell me what the problem is so we can get it out of the way, because I'm exhausted and starving."

He nodded slowly, but she could tell that he was definitely curious. "Okay."

"If I had to guess, you're just waiting for me to break down and turn into a raving bitch throwing my weight around. Like maybe I'll send you out t get gourmet dog food for my Pekinese Pooch name Portia, maybe spelled like the car and not the Shakespeare character, but I prefer the Bard. Or maybe you think I'll send you out to get my laundry."

He didn't say anything, but then again, he looked like he was sitting there surrounded by rattlers, so maybe she was close.

"I'll let you know now that I don't have a dog, I'm not home enough to make it worthwhile for the pet. And I certainly don't need any help picking up my laundry. But," she paused for effect. "I might just ask you to go out and off someone who dishonored my family three generations ago. I can tell you where to bury the body, but I'll deny it if you put me on the stand."

That almost made him crack a smile.

"Seriously. I may have the name that everyone thinks is like the Megabucks Lottery winner, but I'm just a woman, Agent Bravo. That's all you need to know about me."

She watched him as he processed the information.

"Well?" she asked him. "How did I do? Did I get anywhere near the target?"

A low rumbling sound came from his throat. "You're too observant by half, Miss King."

She smiled, pleased with herself. "I wouldn't say that. My teachers used to say I was 'overly talkative' and 'precocious.' My parents took it to mean I was intelligent. Uncle Glen called me a pain in the ass. It's all in how you choose to see it, but I'm just happy to be me these days. Sorry you had to get dragged into this."

He shook his head. "I was just added onto this task force

today. The only thing I've heard about you before is what I saw on the tv and in the newspapers."

She nodded and hissed out a curse. "Big smiles and cocktail dresses looking like I don't have enough cells in my brain to rub together for a spark?"

The laugh that escaped his lips was smothered by a cough. "Nothing quite that bad."

Almost on cue, her belly rumbled, and she grimaced at the definitely unladylike sound.

He smiled, a half-smile, at least from what she could tell with the dark shadows in the car. "We better get some food."

She sighed and relaxed into her seat as he shifted the car into drive. "Good, I'm starved. And before you start up on the restaurant crack from before, I was trying to tell you that I've never been to that hospital before, so I have no idea what's in the area."

"Point taken. I'm sorry about that."

She shrugged. "No biggie. Other people have been bigger jerks than you were."

"Thanks… I think." He started down the street and leaned forward to look out through the windshield. "Hey. I think we're near *Las Quesadillas*. Have you been there before?"

She shook her head and laughed. "Nope, but I'm a girl that likes tortillas and cheese, so if you're promising me lots of that, I'm game."

"Lots of cheese and tortillas. And house made salsa that just might be better than my mom's. Try to tell her that I said it, and I'll deny it to the death."

She held up her hands. "Feed me and you'll have no such problems."

❧

By the time they drove through and ordered enough food to feed him two times over, Vicente was wondering just how much he'd misjudged Sloane King.

No socialite he'd ever been forced to endure would have been caught dead oohing and aahing over *chicharrons*, but when he'd put in an order for himself, she'd given him this puppy dog look as she held up a single finger.

"Uno mas?"

He'd rolled his eyes and ordered a second one.

And when they'd pulled into the parking garage for her apartment he'd tried to hide his shock. He hadn't been to this part of town in a while and he would admit to himself that he'd expected to pull up to a palace, with valets on duty and a concierge service. Not the completely normal apartment complex that they'd driven into.

Vicente knew he had to do a lot of thinking, but first he had to get his head out of his ass.

He followed Sloane's directions and parked in one of the guest spots for the rest of the night.

She gave him a soft smile. "Tomorrow I'll talk to the building manager and see if we can get a spot assigned to you. You'll probably have to explain your requirements."

"Requirements?"

"For what you need to do... your thing."

"Guarding you?"

"Yeah, that."

He grinned at her and she felt a little confused. Didn't he hate her just a little while ago?

"Well, first thing's first. When we get out of the car," he explained, "I'm going to ask you to carry the food. If we were just out together, I'd carry the bags in, but as your guard, I'm going to need my hands free."

"Okay," she replied, still a few seconds behind the conversation, her exhaustion catching up with her, or maybe it was the pain medication they'd given her at the hospital. "I'll carry the food, you watch for the boogeyman."

She heard his soft laughter.

"If it's the boogeyman you're on your own. I'm out of here if he shows up."

She rolled her eyes. "Leave it to me to get the one guard afraid of the boogeyman."

"Hey, I'll take care of the bad guys. I'll even take care of spiders and snakes, but I draw the line at the boogeyman." Almost as if he had to show her how serious he was, he crossed himself and bowed his head.

"Okay," she shifted on the seat, "fair exchange. Now, let's get going, I'm starving."

Taking the large bag into the circle of one arm, she grasped the handle of the drink holder with the other, and when Vicente opened her door and gestured for her to exit, she slid easily to the ground from his SUV.

Tucked into his side as if they were a couple that couldn't quite keep their hands off each other, Sloane let Vicente walk her up to the lobby door.

A wave to the security guard in the lobby had the door unlocked so that Vicente could press his shoulder to the glass and push it open.

"Head for the elevator."

She did as he asked, keeping her gaze focused on the double sliding doors.

Pushing the up button with her elbow she didn't have more than a breath of space before he walked up behind her.

Sloane couldn't see to be sure, but she would have bet all the money in her purse, something around fourty-two dollars, that he was standing directly behind her, shielding her body from the glass windows of the lobby with his own.

It felt odd, really.

But no odder than being shot.

Ah, her little snarky voice popped up, just in case she hadn't been sure that she was too damn tired to function.

Mercifully, the elevator doors opened and it was an empty car.

They stepped inside, Sloane taking the corner when the agent gestured to her.

And he didn't even ask her what floor she was on, just pushed the button. Squeezing her eyes shut against the bright lights, she remembered that she'd told him her address at the hospital.

"Miss King?"

She heard the concern in his voice and lifted her head up a little to see him watching her with concern.

"Are you okay?"

Swallowing to ease the tight feeling in her throat, she gave him a wan smile. "Bone tired," she admitted. "If I'd taken the pain pills earlier at the hospital you would have had to take me out in a wheelchair or a gurney."

He shook his head. "No. Sorry. Draw the line at that. I need my hands free."

Her lips turned down at the corners. "You would have left me there?"

"No."

"Made me walk?" She saw him dart a glance over his shoulder watching the numbers on the wall.

"No."

She pressed her lips together until they made a thin pale line. "Then how would I have gotten home? Hildie drove me to the crash site today?"

He gave her a look that silenced her words. "I would have thrown you over my shoulder and carried you. I told you I need my hands free, remember?"

She swallowed again and nodded. "I remember."

He chuckled. "You're almost adorable tired. I wonder what you're going to be like in the morning."

The door opened and Vicente stepped out into the hallway before gesturing for her to follow him. She moved after him, focused on putting one foot in front of the other.

After looking down both sides of the hallway, he moved off to the right and she followed, still grumbling to herself.

It was childish, and stupid, she told herself. She wasn't that person. But exhaustion had wrung her out, left her aching, and dragging herself down the hall.

When they got to the door, he unlocked it with her key and ushered her just inside the door. She rattled off her alarm code just in case he needed the reminder.

Within seconds, he had the alarm disarmed. He locked the door and they were alone.

Maybe.

"I'm going to check the other rooms. Stay here."

"Mmmm," she didn't get out a word before he moved away toward the hallway.

She knew what he was seeing. Her office, once a spare room that Hildie had stayed in once or twice, and then her bedroom, and its own bathroom.

Simple.

Spare.

Hers.

By the time he came back into the room, he had to take hold of her shoulders and stand her up from where she was leaning heavily against the door.

"Miss King?"

"Mmmhmm?"

"Miss King? Look at me."

She pried her eyes open and looked at him.

"Let's get you to the table."

Nodding, she let him lead her.

The ice in the drinks made little tinkling noises as he took the carrier from her and set it on the table.

She set the bag she was carrying down and looked at the contents. "This is great for me, but where's the food for you?"

"Don't even try it." He chuckled and shook his head. "Make sure you eat before you fall asleep at the table."

She gave him a look and reached into the bag. "I'm tired, not drunk."

She unpacked the food and at one point held up a paper wrapped package and drew in a long breath. "This one's mine."

He chuckled. "It better not be the chorizo. I'll fight you for it."

She held it to her chest and gave him a look. "You could try, G-man, but no one gets between me and food."

She was ready for another snarky comment, instead she turned to look at him in the silence and saw him looking over her body from head to toe and back again.

If it had been a guy off of the street she'd have told him off in a second, but his gaze didn't feel rude or make her skin crawl.

No, he just looked at her as if he was learning something about her and she almost smiled.

"What is it?"

His smile was contagious.

"Just wondering where you put it all if that's the case."

She started to reach a hand down to her backside, but stopped short. "Not going there," she told him.

Shrugging, he reached for one of the wrapped quesadillas. "Pity."

Leaning heavily on the table, Sloane sat down in her chair. "I'm too tired to decide if I'm offended by that remark or turned on."

Opening the waxed paper, she swept her tongue over her

lips and reached for the container of sour cream on the tabletop. It was popped open and set in front of her before she looked across the table and saw that Agent Bravo was watching her carefully.

Narrowing her gaze at him she looked at the wrapped bundle in his hand. "Something wrong?"

He looked from her face and then away toward the wall before he sat woodenly down in the chair opposite her at the table.

"Agent Bravo?" Concerned, she sat the quesadilla back down on the waxed paper. "Is something wrong?"

Leaning back in his chair, he dragged his gaze back up to look at her. "You're surprising me… a little."

"A little?" She rolled her eyes. "I guess I'll have to work harder. *After* I've had some sleep." Picking up her quesadilla, Sloane scooped up some sour cream and took a big bite from the corner. It only took a few seconds for her to get a taste of the whole thing together.

She leaned her elbows on the table and moaned. Managing to lift a hand to cover her mouth, Sloane mumbled out a few words. "So good. What else did you get?"

Sloane wasn't sure, but she thought she heard him grumble under his breath.

"A long sleepless night."

"Okay," she swallowed and took another cream slathered bite, "whatever you say. I, for one, can't wait to get in bed."

❧

Growing up in a large family had done a lot of good things for Vicente while he was growing up. One of the most helpful skills he'd learned throughout the years was being able to fall asleep practically anywhere.

When a couple of cousins stopped in to sleep over at your

already crowded house, you would sleep anywhere you could. Being the eldest boy it was always up to him to corral the younger children during those nights, but he drew the line on the nights when his girl cousins would come over to sleep in Pilar's room.

He'd made the mistake of falling asleep in her room one time.

And woken up the next morning with make up on his face and his nails painted in four different shades of pink.

The skill had served him well on stake outs and protection details. While other agents frowned at the idea of cranking down the back of a bucket seat and taking a good 'power nap' they had only to look at Vicente, happily resting in whatever corner he could find, to decide that he just wasn't human.

That opinion would not have been the case if they had seen him over an hour later.

As soon as Sloane had disappeared into her bedroom, he'd taken the linens that she left for him and improvised a bed.

The sofa was a pull out, but Vicente was normally an easy man when it came to getting some sleep and he didn't want to have to worry about pushing the sleeper back under the sofa cushions in the morning, so he just flopped down and closed his eyes.

Falling asleep was the easy part.

Staying asleep turned out to be the problem.

Startling awake, Vicente checked the time on his phone. Just shy of two in the morning, he closed his eyes and listened carefully to the apartment.

At first it was silent.

Then he heard the rustle of fabric.

Sliding soundlessly from the sofa, he picked up his side

arm from the coffee table and walked across the carpeted floor barefoot.

The sound only intensified as he continued down the hallway.

No one had gotten past him. The alarm was still showing green on the wall.

The windows into Sloane's bedroom were thick solid glass made for insulation. There was no way to open the window from the outside without removing the entire thing or breaking the glass.

That, he would have heard.

Halfway to her bedroom he stopped again.

The sound was coming from her bedroom.

Keeping his back to the wall, Vicente made it the rest of the way to her bedroom door, standing open.

They'd spoken about it before she went to sleep. He'd told her she could shut it most of the way, but he didn't want a locked door between him and his charge, but he also didn't want to have to worry about turning a knob.

She'd shrugged away the worry and told him that she'd leave the door open since the only bathroom was through her room.

Now, he stood on her threshold worried about her.

She was curled up on one side of the queen bed, her arms wrapped protectively around herself. The blankets, all of them were twisted off to the side of the bed or crumbled down at the end.

He had no idea how well she normally slept, but it was obvious that she was in distress.

And he didn't know what he could do about it.

Waking her up seemed like such a personal thing.

They'd shared a late-night meal and she might have flirted a bit with him. She'd been exhausted and injured and out of sorts.

It just didn't seem right leaving her upset and if he were to guess, in pain. She had managed to curl up onto her injured arm.

Shaking his head, he crossed to the bed, picking up a light blanket as he went. He set his side arm down on the nightstand and then took the blanket to the end of the bed and laid it down over the base of the mattress and drew it up over her body while he carefully watched her expression. She didn't seem to notice his presence, he doubted that she knew he was there at all.

He'd covered her with the blanket, so that should have been the end of it. He should have left and gone back to his sofa bed, but Vicente crouched down beside the bed for a moment, wondering if he'd been wrong, if she would manage to settle down on her own.

Before he could come to answer on his own, everything changed.

She gasped in a breath and startled, her expression terrified.

He sat beside her on the bed and touched her shoulder.

Sloane turned and grabbed his arms, almost pulling him off balance. To keep himself from toppling onto her, he reached out and braced a hand on the mattress.

"Miss King, I-"

Her eyes flew open, but he was sure that she was looking right through him. "Hold on. Just hold on a little while longer."

"Okay." Vicente reached out his free arm and took hold of her elbow, holding her as still as he could.

"Don't- don't go."

Vicente knew that she wasn't speaking to him, but he let her hold onto him all the same. There wasn't any harm in it.

Her fingers dug into his arms as tears fell from her eyes,

coursing down her cheek and pooling against the side of her nose. "Promise me."

Lifting a hand, he brushed some errant strands of her dark hair from her forehead before he trailed the knuckles of his hand over the warm curve of her cheek.

Her fingers dug in deeper and even though her nails were trimmed short and close to her fingers, he knew he was going to bruise but it didn't matter.

"Promise me," she demanded, "promise me you'll fight. Hold on."

He ground his teeth together, unsure of what to do. He was there to protect her life. Her heart...

Well, he wasn't sure he was up to the task. He didn't even know who she was talking about. A friend? A lover?

Shifting his grasp, he started to turn her to face the other side of the bed, but she wouldn't let go, so he moved with her. Easing her onto her back, he saw her relax against the pillows.

"Don't leave," her voice was little more than a whisper, "I don't want to lose you."

"Okay," he promised, knowing it was the only way he'd get her to relax, "I won't leave you."

Her fingers softened, her fingers relaxed and slipped free of his arms.

"Good." She let out a long sigh of relief and turned onto her other side, pulling her pillow closer. "I'm so tired of being alone."

A moment later he knew she was fast asleep. The line of her back was a relaxed curve, her toes, visible in the golden pool of light from an outside streetlamp, were relaxed instead of clutched tight as they had been before.

Shaking his head, Vicente reached down to the end of the bed and pulled a blanket back up over her, up to her shoulders.

As he straightened he took a good long look at Sloane King.

He'd grown up seeing her in the newspapers. He'd seen the news when her parents died in a tragic car crash. He'd heard through the law enforcement grapevine when her sister had gotten hooked on drugs, and then he'd seen the headlines when her sister was found dead after being missing for more than a week.

Alone.

She said she was alone, but he wasn't sure what she meant. She had her uncle who was as protective of her as a mama bear with her cubs. She had her friend, Hildie.

When Vicente turned away to walk back into the living room, he stopped short.

Hadn't he just left his family's gathering for much the same reason?

He'd felt alone in the middle of the massive gathering. He knew he was loved and cared for, but it hadn't stopped him from feeling separated.

Vicente knew he didn't have a hope of fixing what hurt in her heart, but he was going to do everything he could to make sure she had time to figure it out for herself.

That, he could do.

CHAPTER 4

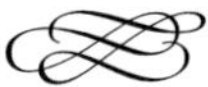

Pulling himself up with a hand on the back of the couch, Vicente grabbed his phone off the coffee table. Squinting at the illuminated numbers, he dropped his forearms to his knees and waited for time to pass.

Yeah, that wasn't going to make it any better.

Getting up on his feet, Vicente walked to the front door and looked out the side window at the sky. It was still dark, but he mumbled to himself. "It's dawn somewhere."

He sighed and turned toward the kitchen. He'd set up the coffee pot the night before, just a heartbeat or two before he fell onto the couch.

He pushed the button with a little more force than he needed to, because 'caffeine.'

By the time he had the pot brewed and a cup poured for himself, he picked up his phone again.

Calling up the phone function, he swept his finger over Cruz's icon and lifted the phone to his ear to wait for the first ring.

The smile on his face was bitterly smug and only grew when he heard a growl on the other end.

"Someone better be dead or dying, Bravo."

"Wanna volunteer?" He pushed his fingers through his hair and curled his toes in the carpet under his feet. "I'm feeling lucky this morning."

There was a long pause and then he heard Cruz's voice again, but louder this time.

"My wife," Cruz's tone was tempered by a softer note and Vicente knew it was his feelings for his wife that bled through his anger at the early hour, "is sleeping. You care to explain why you're calling me?"

"I didn't want to chance Sloane hearing this call."

"The only chance of that is if she's a vampire."

"Living in San Antonio?" The two shared a laugh at the thought. "Seriously, anything new? Do we have suspects?"

"Everything is developing." Cruz sounded a little grumpy, "but with all of the people jumping in on this, I wonder if we're tripping over each other's feet."

"There's no wondering about it," Vicente blew a tentative breath over the top of his coffee cup. "We've got so many LEOs on the street. We're likely driving them deeper underground."

Cruz sighed, and Vicente took a sip and winced at the sudden sting on the tip of his tongue. They both had friends in the local branches of law enforcement, but there was a time when more was too much. "We have to see if we can get the locals to stand down enough that we get a really good look at what's happening here."

"It's not helping that this is a high-profile thing."

"Hmm," Vicente swallowed his first real sip of coffee and felt the caffeine flood his veins, "it does have its drawbacks."

"Did something happen last night?"

Besides Sloane turning his assumptions about her on its head? And the way his grudging respect for her had only grown as he'd done a little internet search on his charge.

If there was a program benefiting women or children in San Antonio, Sloane King had something to do with it.

"'*Cente?*"

"Yeah?"

"You okay? You seem distracted."

What was he going to say to that? He was.

Still, he'd worked with Cruz a number of times over the last few years and there was no need to watch his words with his friend.

"I want to be on the street, Cruz."

Once the words had been said, he relaxed a bit, knowing there was less of a chance that he'd blurt it out at the wrong time.

In front of Sloane.

This was exactly why he didn't do undercover. He ran too hot to bottle things up inside. If he tried, they burst out at the wrong time.

"We've got the street covered, man. You keep her safe."

"I feel like I'm sitting on my hands."

A soft laugh came over the phone. "Careful where you put your thumbs, okay?"

"Smart ass."

A shuffle of sound from the hallway turned his head.

Sloane was leaning heavily on the wall, her eyes half open.

'Hey,' she mouthed.

He nodded at her and lifted his coffee cup, gesturing toward the machine.

She sagged in relief with a smile and managed to push herself away from the wall as she made her way past him to the coffee machine.

He half-turned to follow her with more than just his eyes. Even in her wrinkled scrubs she looked gorgeous. Her hair had been pulled into a ponytail at some point during the night and was now tugged off center, but she didn't seem to care.

He watched as she poured herself a cup of coffee and held it in her cupped hands like the Holy Grail.

Vicente heard Cruz clear his throat. "Yeah?"

"Focus, Bravo."

"Yeah, I'm focused."

"Let me guess, you're not alone."

Damn if Sloane didn't press the side of her coffee mug against her cheek and sigh silently at the feeling.

"Yeah."

"Well, then I'll get off the phone. It's about time to wake up my wife." There was a hint of something softer in his voice and a color to his tone that they were both going to enjoy it.

"Call me when you have an update."

"Sure," Cruz laughed, "let me know when you're in the john and I'll call."

"Jackass." Vicente saw Sloane look up, startled. "If there's an update, call." He was about to end the call when he heard Cruz speak.

"Hey."

"What?" He growled. "My coffee's getting cold."

"Mickie saw the news last night. She wanted me to pass on a message to Sloane. So, can you pass it on or do I have to do it myself?"

Vicente flexed a muscle in his cheek. "Anything for Mickie, Cruz. What's her message?"

"After everything that went down when we met, Sloane's foundation did wonders for her. The group therapy sessions offered by Helping Hearts made all the difference.

"Tell Sloane that Mickie is there. Whatever she needs, just let us know. It's hers."

Setting down his coffee mug, Vicente felt a lump form in his throat. He'd seen his friend back then. Seen the hell he'd gone through when the end of his undercover assignment had ended. Sure, they'd brought down the motorcycle club, but the personal toll had been devastating for his friend and the woman who had captured his heart.

Looking over at Sloane, he watched her climb up onto a stool at the kitchen counter and draw in a sip of coffee like it was life itself.

There was so much more than the image the papers put out. So much more than the pampered princess and socialite. And if nothing else, he owed her the courtesy of delving deeper than the surface. He was going to do better by Sloane.

She deserved that much.

"'*Cente?*"

"Yeah, Cruz. I hear you. Send my love to Mickie."

He ended the call and set his phone down on the counter before he looked up at Sloane.

She was watching him carefully. "Who's Mickie?"

The question startled him a little. It wasn't the question so much but the tone of her voice. It was early. She was still half asleep. The narrowed gaze and watchful eyes made him smile for some reason, but it was the next question that made the corners of his mouth twitch up into a smile.

"Is that what you wore to sleep?"

He looked down at his undershirt and the jogging shorts that he'd pulled out of his car. "They don't issue us a uniform for security details." He shrugged. "And this is comfortable enough. I have to be ready for pretty much anything. Ready to go when I have to."

She ran her gaze over him from head to toe and then looked down at her own clothes. "I remembered thinking that I should change my clothes, but I guess I didn't." She transferred the cup so that she held it with one hand and plucked at the baggy blue of her scrubs top. "I have little snippets of memory from last night after we got here."

That got his attention. "Yeah? What's that?"

"Besides all that cheese I shoved into my mouth?" She laughed and gave him a lopsided grin. "I'm glad these things have an elastic waistband, or I might have split the seams last night."

"Looks like you have some room left."

She rolled her eyes. "Thanks." Sloane yawned, and he had to fight off a yawn of his own. He didn't miss her silent laughter, her shoulders shaking. "You don't have to fight the yawn. I won't think any less of you as an FBI Agent if you can't stifle a natural response. So, you better finish up the rest of that coffee and maybe start on a second cup while I get a shower."

That caught his ear and when she took another sip of her coffee, he leveled a look at her. "If you'd like I can have someone deliver some groceries and I can make you breakfast. We can also have someone bring us pretty much anything you'd like to keep busy. Just let me know what you'd like."

She turned her head slightly to the side and gave him a curious stare. "Keep me busy?" Sloane's laugh was soft, but dry. "I have plenty of things to keep me busy." Looking at the clock above the front door, her lips pursed together slightly. "We've got to get going soon."

Her words registered just as she was walking past him.

"Going? Where?" Snaking his hand around her arm, he pulled her to a stop. "Where do you think we're going?"

Sloane's wide-eyed stare would have been endearing if he wasn't getting ready to strangle her if he didn't get a straight answer.

"Well, I don't know where you are going, Agent." She gave

him a small smirk. "I am going to work. For some reason I thought you were going with me."

❧

She waited. Watching him carefully.

Her uncle Glen had always told her that of the two girls, Kimberly had been the one most likely to touch anything they said was hot. Run out into the street without looking. Snatch up a piece of candy from a store when she just couldn't help herself. But Sloane, he'd tell people, Sloane was the one who held it all in. She took the waves as they kept on coming, bobbing along with it as things happened. But, he'd continue, with a soft rueful laugh, Sloane was the one who was a magnet for misfortune.

When her parents died in the car crash, it was because they were rushing home because she was in the hospital with a high fever. When Kimberly died, it was because Sloane wanted to put Kimberly in an addiction treatment program. He told her that Kimberly ran off to make her sister pay, and died of an overdose.

Oh, her uncle had always stopped short of saying it was her fault, but she just read between the lines, she saw the truth in his eyes. Kimberly had always been his favorite.

Kimberly was the one he took to get ice cream or the circus.

Kimberly was the one who got to play with his silk ties or use his gold pen to doodle on his spare paper.

When Kimberly died, her uncle could barely look at her.

She could feel the warm bite of the agent's fingers on her upper arm, even through the scrubs. He wasn't trying to hurt her, but he wasn't going to let her walk away until he got whatever answer he wanted from her.

She might not know him specifically, but she knew what kind of man he was.

Law enforcement professionals had a certain, straightforward Alpha like quality. Their way or- there was no other way.

Sloane was waiting for Vicente to put his foot down and tell her she was staying in, no matter what.

And then, she was going to put her foot down and tell him where he could put his foot.

She felt his hand ease up around her arm and the sudden shift, even though it was hardly more than a loosening of his grip, made her feel off balance. Wavering, she ended up leaning right back into his hold.

The determined set of his mouth twisted up at the corners and she saw the barest ghost of a smile.

A smile that she was going to hold onto for a while, because, while the serious set of his mouth was imposing, but a real smile, even the littlest smile on his face transformed his stoic expression.

It didn't help that the hand he had on her was connected to a muscled arm the likes of which she'd never seen before. His dark tanned skin in complete contrast to the pristine white tank top that looked like a second skin over his torso.

She'd made some flippant comment before about his sleeping attire, but it had been just that. A throw away comment to deflect from what was really in her head.

It was how she survived.

How she managed to keep a smile on her face during the moments when any real emotion swam up to the surface. It wasn't just pain that scared her, other 'better' emotions scared her just as much… if not more.

It was why her relationship with Hildie was so easy for her. Hildie was everything she wanted to be and not brave enough to do it.

She felt something brush along her arm.

Sloane didn't have to look down to know what it was. His thumb smoothing an arc against her skin.

And heaven help her, if felt so good.

There was a sound, a soft, almost imperceptive sound that must have come from him, she wasn't capable of moving, let alone making any kind of noise.

He caught her gaze with his and she could see the flex and roll of his muscles under his bronzed skin.

All she could do was breathe.

"I can see the wheels in your head turning."

She just hoped he couldn't see exactly what she was thinking. Even she didn't want to examine it too closely.

"I'm guessing that if I told you there's no way in hell I'm letting you out of your apartment, you would have a few choice things to say to me."

She couldn't hold back her own smile.

"Right." He blew out a huff of breath. "I bet you make a lot of people crazy."

"In my time," she managed to make enough sound to be heard, "I've made a few people lose their patience."

His smile widened by degrees. "I bet."

"So," she swept her tongue out over her lips to wet them and saw his eyes dart down to watch, "are you going to tell me that we're stuck here all day?"

His eyes narrowed the littlest bit and she felt as if she were under a microscope.

"I'm almost tempted to say yes, just to see how hot you'd burn."

She heard the words but knew that he didn't mean them the way her mind bent them. Like a pencil in a water glass she knew she was hearing it the way she wanted to hear it.

"Then what?" she asked him. "We patch you up and you take me to work anyway?"

His laughter was warm and came from low in his chest, rumbling up through his body. "You are something, Sloane King. You are most definitely something."

She held her breath, watching him.

Waiting for his decision.

He let go of her arm, stepping back with his hands in the air as if he had to show that he wasn't armed or a danger to her. With a look of mock seriousness on his face, he shook his head.

"I just need you to promise me a few things."

Her laughter brought a smile to her lips. "What exactly am I promising?"

"You stay inside. You stay where I can see you. And if I order you to do something, trust me enough that I'm not doing it for fun or to push your buttons. If I order you to do something, it's because I'm trying to protect your life and by extension, all of the people around you."

She put her hand over her heart. "I promise."

Vicente gestured for her to leave the kitchen. "Go get ready and we'll go as soon as we can."

Sloane added a little more coffee to her cup and started toward the hallway. Just before she disappeared around the corner she heard him call her and she looked back at him.

"Yes?"

"All bets are off if we find out that the shooting was more than just a mistake or random spree and you're actually a target."

The thought sobered her, and she bit into the tender flesh of her bottom lip, nodding. She wanted to do her job. She wanted to help others.

But if they were right and she was a target, then she'd hide.

It wasn't about being afraid for herself.

She'd been so close to death over the years that she almost felt at home this close to the edge, but she would never knowingly put another person in danger because of her.

That she just wouldn't do.

CHAPTER 5

As they drove toward the main Helping Hearts building, Vicente spared a glance at Sloane. Her eyes moved over the passing scenery as if she was familiar with every building and home in the area.

And maybe she was.

"I remember the first time I heard about Helping Hearts Center. I didn't think it would last."

He leaned forward and looked at the crossroad, waiting for a gap in the traffic.

"I hope you didn't lose any money on that bet," she spared him a look before turning back to the street, "If there's one thing I'd like you to learn about me, Agent, is that the best and worst thing you can tell me is that I can't do something." She trailed her fingers along the edge of the doorframe where it touched the window. "I'm stubborn enough to prove you wrong, especially if it's for someone else's benefit."

"Yeah," he barely masked his smile, "they definitely haven't seen you in action."

He thought back to a few editorials that he'd read saying

that Sloane was a publicity whore, that she never met a self-promotion she didn't like.

Even though he'd known her for what amounted to a drop of time in the bucket of her life, he'd seen enough to know that those people probably shouldn't drive, give that they couldn't see what was right in front of their noses.

They'd likely missed the photos snapped of Sloane with her bare hands pressing into the bloody wound on the young officer's chest as he lay bleeding on the asphalt.

He'd driven into this part of town many times over, but most times, it was to investigate a crime, to find those responsible for spilling blood and taking the joy from good people and leaving pain and suffering in their wake.

"You know," Sloane spoke carefully as she looked out the window, leaning her forehead against the glass, "when we opened the center, you would have thought we all had infectious diseases. We couldn't bribe people to come in through the door ."

Vicente pulled his car into the closest parking spot next to the door and set the car in park before he turned to look at her. "Remember what we said?"

Sitting up in the passenger seat, Sloane cleared her throat and held up her hand in the Girl Scout sign. "I, Sloane King, promise to do my best to be a good girl. I won't leave the building without you. I won't leave a room without you," she leaned closer and lowered her voice into a pointed whisper, "although you better not come into the bathroom with me, I draw the line there." Sitting upright again, she continued in her normal voice. "And if you say to hit the floor," she lowered the hand sign to her lap, "I'm on the floor."

He barely kept himself from rolling his eyes. "I'm going to go around-"

"And open the door. Got it."

Vicente managed to get outside the car before he swore under his breath. "Smart ass."

But he couldn't shake the smile from his face, because he had a feeling that the next few hours were going to be… eye opening.

Opening her door, he put his body between the opening and the world around them.

Sloane set one leg on the ground and he clamped his lips together before he turned slightly away, waiting for her to get the rest of her body out of the car. The skirt she'd put on had looked good before they left, he just hadn't realized that when she stepped out of the car she would look more like Dita Von Teese stepping out of a champagne pool. Her leg was long, shapely, and if he was honest it made him sweat.

She cleared her throat and he turned around, only to come nose to nose with her.

Sloane's green eyes were as lush as that leg he'd just committed to memory and the scent he smelled might have been from her shampoo, but he had a feeling it might be the gloss on her lips.

Damn she was close.

And his body knew it.

"Uh," she smiled up at him, "are we waiting for something?"

Shaking his head, he turned around and scanned the area. Nothing seemed out of place. "Okay, let's go." Gesturing ahead, he touched his left hand to her lower back.

❧

The day went by without an issue. Hildie was glad to see her and thankfully her friend remembered about her arm before she wrapped her up in a big hug.

After the first few times that Hildie fanned herself and

mouthed a few comments when he turned his head, Sloane was done with the running gag. Thank goodness Hildie realized it and stopped. It was hard enough trying to get on with business as usual after the wreck the day before.

The odd twinge in her arm when she forgot to take most of the weight with her 'good' side, that was manageable, but it was the emptiness that was bothering her.

Their morning workshop for new mothers was only half its normal attendance numbers and at least two of the women scheduled to come in later in the afternoon had called to cancel their appointments.

By lunchtime, the ache in her arm was also in her stomach. The notoriety of her name was good some of the time.

Sloane feathered her fingertips over her sleeve, feeling the bandage under the fabric only brought flashes of memory rushing back into her head.

"Hey."

She slipped her tongue over her bottom lip, trying to pull herself together.

It wasn't until she felt someone grasp her fingers and pull them away from her arm that she turned.

Agent Bravo gave her a curious look. "Is your arm bothering you?"

She opened her mouth to speak and then stopped, looking down at the way his fingers were holding onto hers, his thumb gently sliding along the side of her index finger.

It was a soothing gesture that she didn't want him to stop. Most people didn't touch her beyond a handshake or a thank you hug from a client.

"Maybe I should take you back to the hospital and have them take a look at you."

He leaned closer and she felt her cheeks warm. Did he have to smell like spices? It was bad enough that he looked the way he looked in that suit, but to look as good as he did and smell like a dream?

"Especially around lunch," she grumbled under her breath.

His eyes narrowed at her. "What was that?"

"I'm sorry, what?" She tried to think of something, anything to get her out of the situation.

"You said something about lunch?"

She grasped at it like a random weed along the top of a cliff, trying to keep herself from going over. "Yeah, lunch… I'm just a little hungry. It's hard to think… when I'm hungry." She sounded like a kid to her own ears, not the calm, capable woman she was normally . "Maybe we should take a break," she suggested, "I'm sure you're hungry too."

He shrugged. "I could eat."

Oh yes, he could.

She hung her head and told her hungry inside voice to take a step off that cliff she was thinking about a moment ago, before it got her in trouble.

"Great," she looked over at her desk and saw her purse beside the phone, "I'll grab my purse and-"

"Sir, I'm sorry, but you just can't walk in there-"

Sloane heard the concerned tone in Hildie's voice.

Vicente must have heard it too because he stepped between her and the doorway, his focus squarely on the empty space.

Hildie was a step behind the man in a suit and a step in front of his cameraman. "Sloane, I'm sorry. I couldn't stop him."

Sloane hated to admit it, but she knew who the reporter was. He loved a good juicy story and didn't mind making up stuff if it suited him. The easiest way to make sure that you were the center of his life for a few days was to try to avoid him.

And avoiding him was going to be the last thing she could do at the moment.

Pasting a smile on her face, she stepped around Vicente after giving him a reassuring pat on his arm. Walking toward the reporter, she held out her hand and greeted him with more enthusiasm than she felt.

"Jordan Carson! How are you doing?"

He looked a little uncomfortable in his tweed jacket and the overly done make up on his face. Even though the room was airconditioned, he was sweating profusely as he reached her. "I am well, Miss King. So delightful to see that you are back on your feet after your horrible injury."

The camera man pointed the lens straight at her face and so she schooled her expression into one of calm and the hint of a sunny smile. "What I suffered was just a scratch, Jordan. I-"

"I'm surprised to see you here at your little venture when, from what I heard, you should still be in a hospital bed, recovering from your injury."

"As you can see," she lifted up both arms and gestured at the room in general, "I'm fine. And Helping Hearts is open. All our groups are meeting, and classes are happening. And if there are any women or children in your audience in need of help, we are here and ready to help them."

Jordan's smile faltered a bit, but since he wasn't in full view of the camera. "Oh, well, that sounds like you're getting over your injury quite well."

"My injury really wasn't much of anything, Jordan. A little bit of blood and a few stitches and-"

"Goodness," he gasped in a breath, "that sounds horrid!"

Sloane tilted her head to the side and gave him a concerned look. "Maybe you should sit down, Jordan." Gesturing to a chair, she gave him a sympathetic smile. "Then I can tell you about the young Police Officer who was gravely injured yesterday. His mother, a sweeter woman you'll never meet, is camped out at his bedside waiting for her son to heal up. They're all the family they have in the world and she's so proud of his job with the San Antonio Police Department." She spoke about the two and tried to get across the true heart of the situation that mother and son now faced. "When Officer Kelly is released and sent home, he's going to need a lot of care and his mother will need help."

Turning to look for Hildie, Sloane saw her friend step up beside the cameraman. "I'll have my assistant give you a contact phone number and email addresses. The Kellys will have local help from their community, but donations are also welcome. In fact, I'll be happy to add you to the donors list. After we're done filming, I'll have you fill out a form. I'm sure your viewers will admire your community spirit."

Jordan cleared his throat. "Well thank you for taking the time to speak to us, Miss King. That was very informative. We'll be sure to get the word out."

❧

Vicente unhooked the button at the waist of his suit coat and draped the garment over the back of the couch after he slid it off his arms. Sitting down on the comfortable cushions, he pulled out his phone.

A text message from Cruz made him regret ever giving the man his phone number.

YOU LOOK GOOD ON TV

There was a link in the next message.

Steeling himself, Vicente clicked on the link and waited for the video to load.

It was the news segment filmed at the Helping Hearts Center and there he was, standing behind Sloane. If he'd had any clue that the cameraman had included him in the shot, he would have moved away.

"It's a good thing I don't work undercover." Having his face in a video like this would make it impossible.

He was ready to close the app on his phone and send a message back to Cruz when he stopped his finger over the X. He watched the clip that they posted online and then watched it again.

It wasn't easy given that he'd been there the whole time and seen the whole uninvited interview. What they'd put online was barely an eighth of the interview. Realistically, it happened. He knew it, but the way this Jordan guy had cut the piece together, there was hardly anything he recognized.

It gave him a fresh perspective on her life.

He didn't think reporters would ever want to do a story about him, but if they butchered things the way this hack did to what Sloane said, he would have their butts in a sling.

How did she deal with this?

He thought back to all the stories he'd seen about her on television throughout the years. All the seemingly inane answers that she'd given. How many times had he formed an opinion about her not because he knew anything about her, but by what the media had reported? How many times had there been a 'real' story behind the fluff that they posted about Sloane.

It didn't make sense.

It wasn't about sense.

It was about sensation.

He decided not to reply to Cruz. Instead, he just shut off his phone and tossed it onto the couch cushion beside him.

He owed Sloane an apology, but it just seemed too odd to talk about it now. How was he going to explain how long he'd judged her for nothing more than what was said about her?

Sinking down a little on the couch, he waited for her to come back from her bedroom so they could discuss her schedule. After getting a feeling for what it was like on a given day, he knew they'd need to talk about what they could do to protect her and allow her to continue her work. He knew he wasn't going to convince her to put it on hold until they had definite proof that she wasn't in danger.

"Agent Bravo, I-"

Startled, he turned on the couch, dropping one arm on the back as his eyes took her in. She'd come back into the room silently. Light feet on carpeting would do that he guessed.

His eyes roamed over her, struggling to understand what it was he was looking at. "What is that?"

She paused for a moment, narrowing her eyes at him as if she was trying to decipher a foreign language. "What is what?"

Pressing two fingers to his temple, Vicente muttered under his breath while he collected his thoughts. "I thought you were getting ready for… ready to sleep."

Shifting from one foot to the other, she set her hands on her hips. "I did, and this," she gestured along the side of her body from her chest to her waist, "is what I normally wear to bed."

All he could see was a shiny robe with sleeves that hung down to her wrists and a bottom hem that barely… barely made it to the middle of her thighs.

And those thighs.

He'd seen her legs earlier, but thighs?

Long, shapely, and colored like peaches and cream down to her pale pink toenails. The air he'd had in his lungs fled like his good sense, leaving his chest tight and other parts of him aching and uncomfortable.

"*Madre de dios*! How about wearing some pants?"

"You're actually going to tell me what to wear in my own apartment?" Her laughter wasn't anything more than a huff that kind of sputtered from her lips. "That's not going to work."

"No," he turned the tables on her, "that outfit isn't going to work."

She stared back at him with a curiously calm expression on her face. "You are the one who basically moved into my apartment. You can tell me where I can and cannot go. What I can and cannot do 'outside' these walls, but can you explain how what I wear in my apartment has anything to do with my security?"

He had no answer for her. It was an irrational outburst, but it was what it was.

Sitting there, looking up at her, watching her turn in one direction and then another, the hem of her robe fluttered just enough to take his breath. That teasing scrap of silk she'd tied around her body stole his sanity in one wavering movement.

Under her robe, Sloane King, was wearing something even shorter. If she sat down on the sofa beside him, there was no way he'd be able to pay attention to anything about her schedule. All he'd think about would be something completely inappropriate.

Like how her thighs would feel under his hands.

Facing down criminals?

Not a problem.

Plush thighs and eyes full of challenge?

He couldn't seem to turn his mind away from the

thoughts of her, and those shapely legs, and everything else in between, out of his head.

Blowing out a breath, Vicente shook his head. "I should have been more specific."

It didn't help that his admission changed her expression from a bit of consternation to an almost smirk that had him wanting to kiss it off.

Well, the smile… and maybe the rest of her clothing.

"Look," she drew his attention back with a softer tone of her voice, "I'm sorry if I'm being a bit stubborn. It's been a long day for me, but I'm sure it's been just as long for you. So, if it will make things easier, I'm going to go and change."

He leaned his head back against the cushions. "Thank you."

Closing his eyes, he waited for the next onslaught on his senses. All he had to do was get through one talk and go to sleep.

Start the torture all over again in the morning.

This was supposed to be simple. Protect his charge. Keep her alive, and then move on to the next job.

He'd done it a hundred times. Solve the crime… move on. Find the kidnap victim… move on.

But Sloane. She was temptation.

She was walking, talking frustration.

The couch cushion beside him sank the slightest bit and he turned his head, cracking open one eye to see what she'd done to drive him insane.

And he wasn't disappointed. She was one step away from a homemade hazmat suit. Thick socks, sweatpants and a sweatshirt that looked several sizes too big, a scarf that almost covered her mouth and a knit cap that was pulled on so tight it looked like a shower cap. In a word she was… overboard.

His sigh made her smother a laugh, and when his hand hit

the cushion beside his thigh with a heavy thump, she jumped to her own defense.

"I'm covered." She gestured at herself. "From my ankles all the way up to my nose. I'll even stand up, so you can measure the length. Or I'll hold my hands at my sides and you can see that it's longer than my fingertips. Would that make you happy?"

"If I give you my gun, will you put a bullet through my head and end my pain?"

"I never knew that FBI Agents were so fatalistic... and afraid of women."

That got him.

Both eyes were open and narrowed on her. He turned and toed off his shoe before drawing his leg up onto the sofa cushion. "I'm not afraid of women."

Her look called him a liar.

"I have a job to do."

"Then do it, but you're on my ground. In my apartment, Agent Bravo," she clipped the syllables to enunciate her words, but she didn't seem the least bit cowed by his presence or his building frustration. "It's not like I'm walking around here naked. If there is someone out there trying to harm me, can I at least wear something comfortable at home? I'm sure my uncle will have them dress me up like a porcelain doll if they managed to shoot me. Until then, this apartment is supposed to be my sanctuary. My place to just be... me. I swear to you," she sighed, "I'm not trying to be annoying. I think it just comes naturally. Some people just don't like me.

"I'm sorry that you're one of them. I wish I knew what to do to make it better, but I've never been able to meet everyone's expectations. I don't see how I'll start now."

He heard the soft scratch of her voice in her throat, saw

the hesitant brush of her hand on her thigh, skimming the folds of those ridiculous sweatpants.

She had a point. A good one.

She wasn't in prison. This wasn't house arrest.

He was tasked to protect her.

What difference did it make what she wore? If she was safe, then he should suck it up.

Deal with it.

Take care of her instead of treating her like she was his partner in a stakeout.

It wasn't her fault that he was barely keeping his hands to himself. That every time he caught a glimpse of her legs and the firm curve of her backside, he wanted to peel off every inch of her clothing and cover her with his body, his hands, and his mouth.

"You're right," he hated to make the admission, because the instant he'd opened his lips, he'd wanted to confess what he felt- no, what he needed from her. "This is your apartment. And for now," he managed another breath, "we're here to keep you not just safe, but I'll try not to drive you crazy."

Leaning her cheek on her hand she sighed. "Too late."

A moment of silence fell between them before she reached out her hand and laid it on his arm. "I've been on my own for quite a while. So, this is kind of odd for me. I know I live in Texas and my college roommate did have a concealed carry permit, but this," she gestured at his shoulder holster, "is all new to me. I'll try," Sloane's pointed look held more than a hint of humor, "but that's the most I can guarantee."

He looked down at her hand on his arm and tried not to flex his forearm against her touch. It was electric. It was warm and inviting.

Suddenly, the couch was too small.

Sloane was too close.

And his clothes were too tight.

He was a hairsbreadth away from stripping that whole pile of clothing off of her body and pulling her into his lap, just so he could taste her lips.

Trace the seam with the tip of his tongue.

Fist his hand in her hair and pull her flush against his chest.

Need.

The need he felt almost obliterated his control.

"So," she whispered the word and her fingers shifted against his arm, tracing his skin with fire from her tentative touch, "you wanted to talk about my schedule?"

Salvation.

And disappointment.

It was going to be a hell of a long, hard, night.

Again.

❧

On my own two feet.

Sloane woke up with her motto on repeat in her head.

It was the thought that wheedled its way into her head the day after she'd lost her sister. All she wanted to do was lay in bed and stare at the wall. She'd handled becoming an orphan with grit and determination. She'd managed to hold herself together because Kimberly seemed wholly incapable of doing so.

Papers had to be signed. Business taken care of. And as much as she loved her sister, even Uncle Glen who loved Kimberly best, knew that Sloane was better equipped to take care of the cold and impersonal things that came with a death in the family.

But was she the best choice?

It turned out it didn't matter, she was the only one able to lock away the mind-numbing pain and put a pen to paper, make the arrangements, and talk to the press.

"The world," Uncle Glen had reminded her enough times to commit it to memory, "was waiting to hear about the Kings."

And there were times. Many, many times. That Sloane just wanted to tell the world exactly where to step off. That the ache in her chest and the dull throb in her head was just that.

Hers.

The world could… well there weren't polite words that truly explained what was in her head.

When Kimberly died, the ache had gotten worse, the throbbing in her head sounded like a jack hammer 24/7.

And yet, the world needed an update on the tragedy that was the King family.

Waking up on her back. Her covers thrown to the floor. And her eyes gritty from the tears she'd shed the night before.

The talk with Agent Bravo- Special Agent Vicente Bravo- had gone well. He'd relaxed around her in some ways. Maybe it was his time at the center.

Most people gave her the 'aww, you poor little rich girl' look and that was it. Yet, sometime during their day together, he'd loosened up a bit, relaxed the hard line of his shoulders, and given her a smile that didn't look like it was FBI issue for difficult subjects.

And it had changed the way she looked at him too.

Yes, Sloane King was just as shallow as the average person. She judged others like they judged her, only she had to keep her feelings under lock and key, because, "Cameras are everywhere."

But somehow, they'd broken the ice between them and when Agent Bravo looked at her she knew he didn't see her as the spoiled rich girl he'd expected.

And if her life didn't already suck more than the average bear's, during their conversation about his work regarding her case and her schedule that she couldn't give up, she'd found herself totally, stupidly, attracted to him.

Complications.

She needed them like a hole in her already empty heart.

Besides, she told herself last night when she'd laid in bed, it was a one-way thing. Totally safe.

Like the way she had a thing for Oded Fehr from the Mummy films. She could have a healthy, or at least she hoped it was healthy, fantasy life with the gorgeous and mysterious Medjai warrior, and it didn't hurt anyone.

Sure, she'd spent a few dollars here and there on batteries. But that was normal.

Right?

Shifting onto her side, Sloane reached off the edge of the bed and managed to pick up her blanket off the floor. Dragging the light cotton blanket over her body, she turned her back to the door and tried to lie still.

Tried to blank out her mind.

Yeah, that wasn't going to work.

The ache she'd felt only the stirrings of the night before, was back with a vengeance. It hadn't helped that she'd been the one to think about him. Like conjuring a demon on a supernatural television show, or that ghost story about the girl in the mirror, she'd brought him up in her thoughts and that had sent blood coursing through her veins.

And with that rush, came others. Hormones and all kinds of tingling feelings that she really didn't have time for.

Not with the object of her potential fantasies in the next room and her door, damn her, open because when she'd purchased the condo she'd gone with one just a step or two above a studio. Almost two bedrooms and a bathroom was more than enough for her, but never in her wildest dreams had she ever thought she'd had a temporary bodyguard asleep on her sofa.

Correction.

Sprawled on her sofa.

She'd made the mistake of going to get a bottle of water from the kitchen and there he was. One leg over the arm of the couch, the other foot on the floor, the blanket he'd covered up with haphazardly draped over him, more off than on.

Blankets were wasted on them, she'd thought, they both kicked them off every night.

And that made her pick up two bottles of water instead of one.

And then, lying in her bed, covered with her blanket for at least a few moments, she'd let herself imagine.

Let herself dream.

Her thigh draped over his. One arm tucked under his shoulder, the other held in his secure grasp. His thumb smoothing over her palm as he kissed her, smothering any kind of protest, not that she was planning to.

Her breaths shortened and seemed to fill her ears in the silence of the room. If just the thought of touching him, having him touch her, made her toes curl and her skin heat even in the cool air-conditioned bedroom, she knew she was a goner.

And that ache within her wasn't about her heart, it was all about the parts of her that were instinct, and instinct was the last thing she trusted.

Then why, she wondered, was it so easy for him to get under her skin? How, in just a few hours, had he worked her defenses loose?

And why did her breath catch, and her nipples tighten, as she worked a hand under the waistband of her pants and down between her legs… all because she imagined it was him.

It was Vicente Bravo, a man who'd walked into her life and shaken everything loose.

CHAPTER 6

The next morning had started off on an odd foot, thanks to Sloane. And she knew it.

She'd woken up a good hour before her alarm, her hand under her sleep shirt, smoothing over her belly and working its way up to her breast.

She kept quiet, pressing her teeth and her lips together, as she'd feathered a slight touch over her nipple. From there, it had gone downhill, or just down, working her way past the waistband of her leggings.

It was a heady thing. A stolen moment of passion, even if it was DIH: Do it Herself.

Sloane could count the number of men she'd slept with on one hand, the number of times she'd managed an orgasm during sex on one finger.

There just hadn't been a man that satisfied both the need in her body and her heart.

Her fingers faltered as she replayed that thought over again. The man in the next room had nothing to do with her heart.

Right?

Her fingers curled at the tips and brushed through her folds, eliciting a soft sigh from her lips. Yeah, nothing but physical right here. Nothing but a little tension and a bit of stress, and, "ah."

It was just enough of a building release to make her toes curl up as her nerves tingled in places she'd forgotten existed.

It was just enough to remind her of what she'd been missing.

And just enough-

"Miss King?"

His voice was much too clear to be in the next room. It sounded more like he was-

"Are you okay?"

Thank goodness she was facing away from the door. Not that he would have been able to see her in the dark, but still, she had her back to him and that was enough to help her lie.

"Fine. I'm fine. Everything is fine."

"Okay, I just thought I heard something."

She bit down on her lower lip, using the pain to focus her thoughts. "I had a cramp."

It was close enough to the truth.

"Okay," he hesitated. "If your arm is hurting you, I can take a look at it."

So helpful. But what she'd been moaning about had nothing to do with her arm. Just her hand. A few fingers. And a libido that had been asleep too long for her own good.

She had to get herself together.

"I'm fine, thanks." Her voice was tight, just a little bit of a gasp in the tone, but that was better than the whimper she was holding back.

The silence in their conversation grew.

"Okay, I'm going to go back to the couch. Let me know if there's anything I can do for you."

She swallowed down a few choice suggestions, all of them involved him giving her a hand… or two.

There was probably some kind of law about that. Tempting an FBI Agent into dereliction of duty.

But, all Sloane offered up was a simple. “Thanks, I will.”

When she finally emerged from her room, she found her couch empty. The blankets had been folded away and stacked at the end.

“Agent Bravo?” Even as she called for him, she knew he was gone. The room felt empty and cold.

Even the warm pot of coffee that he’d brewed didn’t do much to pick up her spirits.

A movement outside the door caught her attention and she took a few steps to the side to look out through her curtains.

There was a San Antonio Policeman on her door.

There was more than a hint of relief that coursed through her veins at the sight, but also a bit of disappointment.

She moved to the door, keyed in her code to unarm the system, and opened it carefully. The officer on the other side watched her with open curiosity.

“Good Morning, Ma’am.”

“Morning, Officer.” She watched him reach up a hand and tug on the front brim of his hat.

“Agent Bravo told me to let you know he was called into the FBI Field Office. They think they have a line on one of the men involved in the shooting.”

“Oh, good,” she grabbed on to the door in relief and told herself there wasn’t any need to be sad about the news at all. “Sorry you had to draw the short straw and get watch duty.”

He shook his head and gestured in her direction. “Proud to help, Miss King. I had a family on my beat, domestic disturbance calls almost every few days. During one of our calls, my partner gave the wife one of your cards and encouraged her to call."

Sloane placed a hand over her heart and waited for the rest of the story. So many of them didn't end well.

"The woman's husband came home drunk one night and tried to shove her through a window. The bastard- umm sorry, the husband tripped over his own feet and went through the window himself. Helping Hearts helped the woman get back on her feet, gave her job training and helped her find a nearby foodbank that helped her until she could manage for herself."

Sloane felt her eyes well up with tears. "I hope she's doing well now."

Grinning, the officer set his hands on his hips and nodded. "The whole family is doing well, and they owe it all to you."

She shook her head, waving off the compliment. "So many people volunteer and help, it's not fair to put it on my shoulders." She thought for a moment. "I would like to know the name of your partner, so I can thank them and get them as many referral cards as they need."

The elevator door opened, and Sloane tensed, pulling herself slightly behind the heavy door for protection.

The officer beside her barely touched his hand to his weapon when he dropped it again. "Don't worry, Miss King," he gestured toward the oncoming figure, "that's my partner, Pilar."

The woman walking toward them was petite, but Sloane bet that had no bearing on her ability to do her job. Just like the no nonsense set of her features didn't change how beautiful she was. She didn't wear a uniform, but the jeans and blouse she wore graced her figure well.

Pilar handed her partner a coffee and gave him a wink. "You've got the door, Manfredi. I'm still on vacation."

Sloane stepped back and opened the door without being asked and Pilar's smile set her at ease.

"I brought something for breakfast," she tilted her head and gave Sloane a once-over. "You and I are going to have a little talk."

Sloane waited until Pilar had set down the box in her hand to close the door. "Should I be worried?"

The smug smile on Pilar's face made Sloane smile, it was that infectious. "No reason to worry," she used her fingernail to sever the tape holding the box closer, "I come bearing pastries and I have a teeny tiny favor to ask."

"Okay, what do you need, Officer-"

"Bravo," she grinned, "Officer Pilar Bravo. Vicente is my brother."

❧

When he got back to Sloane's apartment building he chose to take the stairs. Hoofing it up the three flights was unnecessary, but it felt good. The stretch of muscles in his thighs help to counteract the metaphorical spanking he'd just received from the Mayor.

He'd gone in to speak with his boss about developments in the case, but Director Travis wasn't alone. The Mayor had decided to attend the meeting. It was strange enough having him in the room, but as soon as the Director delivered his news with his jaw nearly locked in frustration, the Mayor had lit into them both.

"You were waiting?"

Director Travis had tried to step in, but Vicente was more than willing to take the hits. "Sir-"

"What did you think you would accomplish by waiting? Give the... give the criminals another chance to kill her?"

Vicente shook his head. "We took every precaution, sir. Miss King has had a guard around the clock. Top of the line security. She has continued her valuable work-"

"And just how," the Mayor spat the words at him, "would she be able to continue her 'valuable work' if someone killed her?"

"No one is going to-"

"She's the last of her family, Agent! The very last of the Kings in her line. If you let something happen to her, I can assure you that you'll lose your job."

Director Travis had tried to step in and put the Mayor on notice, but Vicente didn't let him.

Vicente had a few words of his own to say.

"If something happens to Sloane, be assured that you won't have to take my job. I'll lay down my own life before I allow something to happen to her." Into the silence, he'd ended their meeting. "If you'll excuse me, Sir. I need to get back to my charge."

All the way back to Sloane's apartment his mind was working on overtime. He was going to have to move her to a different location. He was going to have to do a lot of things he knew she'd fight.

But he'd been completely honest with the Mayor. He was going to do what he had to. He just had to figure out a way to soften the blow.

If there was one thing he knew about Sloane King, it was that she didn't just see her work as work. She saw her work as her life. Her mission.

And if anyone could understand that, it was him.

He just had to get her to put it on hold long enough to make sure she could continue to do her work for another sixty or seventy years.

He just didn't know how.

. . .

The officer at the door gave him a nod and a report. "All's quiet on the home front, sir. Hardly a peep ."

That drained the smile right off his face. "What the hell does that mean?"

Clearing his throat, the officer couldn't seem to meet his eyes. "Another officer stopped by to see Miss King."

The man on the door swallowed so hard that Vicente was worried he might choke on his own tongue.

"And *who* was this officer?"

No one was scheduled to come by beside Officer Manfredi who was standing in front of him.

"Your sister. Pilar."

Taking the key ring from his pocket, Vicente opened the apartment door and shut it behind him a moment later before keying in the code to deactivate the alarm.

He continued to face the door when he spoke. "Miss King-"

"Oh," she sighed, "don't you think we're a little past that formal greeting?"

Turning around to face her, he sighed. "Sloane-"

"Vicente," she replied with a pleasant smile on her face, "what do you do when you're not protecting the endangered socialites of San Antonio?"

He stopped tugging at his tie. She had an arm on the back of the couch and she was watching him with a spark of curiosity in her eyes. "Why do I get the feeling that this is a trick question?"

"What do you like to do in your spare time?"

She gave him a pointed look and he wondered what he'd done now.

"This is a trick question." He widened his stance and stared back at her. "Go ahead, do your worst. Just get it over with."

Rolling her eyes, she leaned forward and gave him a secretive smile. "Were you going to tell me that you have a family engagement that you're supposed to go to tonight?"

"I told my *Tia* that I was working." He shook his head. "How the hell did you find out?"

She shrugged at first and then gave him a pointed look. "Your sister ratted you out."

He stared at her with a wicked grin. "That's why she came to see you."

"Of course she came by. And before you get all upset about it, we exchanged numbers," she clarified. "She wanted me to have someone to call when I wanted to strangle you. Apparently, she's more concerned with me going to jail for attempted murder than keeping your secret about the party."

His lips pressed tightly together and folded his arms across his chest. "Pilar sold me down the river."

Sloane's laugh was soft and warm. "In a heartbeat."

"I'm not sure I like the two of you being friends," his voice was almost a growl and he swore it made her smile more.

"We're not friends so much as in a mutual 'make your life hell' society."

His head dropped down until his chin touched his chest. "Well congratulations, you two certainly know your stuff."

"Child's play." She gave him a dismissive wave of her hand. "Go get changed."

Startled, he narrowed his gaze at her. "What did you say?"

She tilted her head to the side as she looked at him. "I said to 'go get changed.' If you don't want to change, I guess you can go like that."

"Go like what?"

Sighing, she narrowed her gaze at him. "To the party, Special Agent." Shaking her head, she gave him a half-hooded look. "You're sure pretty to look at, but I'm worried that your mind is going."

When he didn't move, she did.

He watched her slide off the couch and gracefully get to her feet. The black wrap dress she wore had no sleeves, but it was held up by two tiny straps over each shoulder. Her wound had been dressed with a new bandage that almost matched the tone of her flesh, but he doubted anyone would be looking at the wrap.

As she rounded the side of the couch the overlapped edge of her skirt waved and twisted with her stride and he saw a flash of red.

Sloane wore her long sable hair in a knot at the nape of her neck and there wasn't any sign of jewelry on her ears, neck, or arms.

With just a hint of make-up on her skin, she glowed with her lips curved into a taunting smile as she sauntered up to him. "I'm told you're a good dancer, Vicente." She stopped and gave him a look from head to toe. "Afraid you'll disappoint?"

He felt her eyes on him and mentally swore at his sister. Sloane may joke about putting him through hell, but this was a lifelong game with his sister.

And Pilar loved to get the upper hand.

"When I get you on the dance floor, Sloane," he licked his bottom lip as his eyes made their own head to toe survey of his charge. Sure, he'd seen the hair, make-up, and dress already, but it wasn't until he got down to her feet that he saw how much trouble he was in, "you won't have any questions about how good I am."

He wasn't a man that liked really high heels. Too many women favored them for the look, but there was a certain height of heel for each woman where it made walking safely an impossibility and he was a man that liked to dance.

Sloane's heels weren't higher than three inches. The

strappy shoes glittered in the lamp light, crossing over the arch of her foot to hold the shoe securely, but it was the shiny red paint on her nails that hit him below the belt.

For one brief agonizing moment, he had an image in his head of the black heels of her shoes digging into the backs of his thighs.

He was hard in a moment, his breath catching in his lungs.

If he wasn't careful, he was going to reach out a hand and tug on the bow she'd tied near her waist and see exactly what she had on under that clingy little dress.

He didn't even meet her eyes before he moved. He couldn't, knowing what she'd see in them if he did. Instead, he reached up a hand and whipped off his tie, tossing it onto the back of the sofa.

Wrapping his hand around hers, he tugged her toward the door and they were off.

❧

She could hear the party before they could see it. Leaning forward in her seat, she looked over the dashboard and saw that the street was clogged with cars and people milling about.

Falling back against her seat, Sloane sighed.

Beside her in the driver's seat, Vicente laughed, earning himself a hard look from his passenger.

"Let me guess," his voice was soft, and smooth, "you're worried we're going to miss the fun?"

"We did get a late start." Leaning her head back against the seat wasn't easy with the chignon that she'd styled at the nape of her neck, so she turned her head to look at him. "And I did kind of strong arm you to come."

Looking at his profile with the soft streetlights gilding his strong silhouette in a golden hue, she was stunned. She was used to the hard, angular lines of his face and the bronzed perfection of his skin but seeing the indulgent smile on his strong lips warmed her skin even with the car's AC on.

"I wanted to go to the party," his admission was hushed as if he wasn't sure he wanted to voice it, "but I didn't think you'd want to go." He cleared his throat. "I don't think I've seen you at a community center in the society pages."

She bit back the response that was on her tongue. They were getting along and as much as the assumption had stung, she could see where his perception came from. It just didn't make it hurt any less.

"Hey."

She blinked her eyes a few times to clear the hint of tears that were threatening to ruin her mood.

"Sloane?"

Before she could turn her head to look back through the windshield, she felt the crook of his finger under her chin, and the pad of his thumb brush the underside of her lip.

"What happened just now?"

It would be so easy to paste a smile on her face and blow it off, but she'd hoped that they were beyond her image by now.

"It happens, you know?"

She sat silently for a minute, struggling to put her thoughts to words.

"What you see in the paper is what they want to show. They want to show the big names in the paper and that means that I'm in there from time to time.

"But the name doesn't mean the same thing to me. The name means that I'm the last of an era. It means that I've lost every single blood member of my family.

"I know it doesn't seem like it from the papers and the media coverage, but most of my time I'm at those community centers, the clinics, the shelters.

"I hope you see more to me than those pictures. If not," she sighed and felt the ache in her chest deepen, "then I don't know why you would bother to watch my back."

She turned, pulling away from his hand and looking out the passenger side window.

The playful mood in the car was gone and she blamed herself for the loss. She should have let it roll right off her back and made a stupid joke like she did whenever anyone made comments about her *larger than life* existence, but Vicente's words had cut deep.

She heard his soft exhale and hoped that he wasn't getting ready to turn the car around and go back to her apartment. She really wanted him to be able to celebrate with his family. Taking care of her didn't have to mean that he put his life on hold.

"Sloane, I-"

"*Tio* V!" The excited shout was followed up by a hailstorm of knocks against the driver's side window.

Sloane turned to look and saw three faces peering in through the glass. One of them was still tapping at the glass.

"*Hola, Tio*!"

Toggling the switch, Vicente's window opened and the three jostled each other.

"Do your parents know where you are?"

She heard the cautionary tone of his voice and heard the answering laughter of the kids outside.

"*Tia P* told us to watch out for you and your *friend*." The answer was followed by a chorus of giggles and the shortest 'head' of the trio came with an arm that waved at her. "*Hola, Tio's friend.*"

The infectious humor eased the tension from Sloane's shoulders.

The tallest and likely the eldest of the group wedged himself into the center and laid both of his forearms on the open window bottom. "You want me to park your car?"

She heard the hopeful, almost begging tone in the boy's voice.

Vicente tilted his head to look the boy square in the face. "Show me your license."

One arm disappeared from view and popped back with a rectangular card held like the Holy Grail between the boy's fingers. "Here you go, officer."

The children on either side of him laughed as Vicente leaned closer to his nephew. "That's Special Agent to you, young man."

With a nod and quick flick of his hand, the boys stepped back and away, leaving Vicente room. The car was put in park and he got in on his side. Just as Sloane unbuckled her seatbelt, her door was opening.

Vicente was waiting for her, his hand extended, and the tension in her body shifted. Worry and disappointment lost their hold for a moment and when she set her hand in his, he gave her fingers a gentle squeeze.

Leave it to Vicente to twist her heart around in her chest in a heartbeat.

Sloane stepped out of the car and barely had a second to breathe before the younger boys dashed past them and closed the door.

Tucking her hand into the crook of his arm, Vicente set off at an easy pace toward the sounds of the party ahead of them.

. . .

By the time they made it to the side of the birthday girl, Sloane had been introduced to more than a score of Vicente's relatives. Her head was fairly swimming with names and faces.

As they moved through the throngs of people on the dance floor, Sloane latched a hand onto his forearm hoping she wouldn't lose him in the crowd.

He reached his arm back and took hold of her other hand. "Don't worry," he called back through the din of the dance music, "I won't lose you." He gave her hand a squeeze. "Come on, I think I see Blanca."

When they arrived at the center of the floor, Sloane didn't need to ask which young girl was Blanca Bravo, Vicente's eldest niece. Her dress wasn't just a dress, but a gown. Swathed in yards and yards of organza ruffles, the petite young woman looked like an antebellum pixie with an addiction for ringlet curls.

Vicente called out to his niece, but the noise made it nearly impossible to turn her head.

Luckily, Pilar was standing beside her niece and gestured for her to turn around.

Sloane was nearly knocked off her feet a moment later. The wide circumference of her hoop skirt kept everyone at a certain distance, but she still managed to loop her arms around her uncle's neck.

"*Tio* V! You came!"

Laughing, Vicente managed to stretch his arms long enough to hug her back even with the layers of organza and crinolines between them.

He spoke softly into her ear and then the two shared a laugh with each other. Blanca glowed with love for her uncle.

Sloane swallowed and blinked back sudden tears. Family.

The Bravos had enough members of their family to found

their own town if they had a mind to, but it wasn't just their numbers, it was the love they showed each other. The love they felt for each other.

She hadn't had that in quite a while.

Sloane lifted her hand to brush away a tear and felt herself tugged sideways. When she came to a stop she found herself anchored to Vicente's side, his hand on her hip.

"Blanca, this is-"

"Sloane King!"

Sloane cringed at the breathy tone in the teenager's voice.

"I know!" Blanca reached out and grabbed both of Sloane's hands. "You came to our school and talked about safety and what to do if we're ever harassed or feel unsafe. All my friends talked about it for days. We still check with each other and make sure to follow your hints when we're not together. Wow." Blanca darted a look at her uncle and then looked at Vicente's hand on her hip before meeting her eyes again. "Are you dating my *tio*?"

Before Sloane could manage to even process the question, all of Blanca's friends crowded in after her squeal of happiness blasted straight through the music of the party.

Suddenly, she was the center of attention and all the teenage girls were going wild with laughter and cheers.

She leaned her shoulder closer to Vicente. "Do something?"

He shrugged, and she looked up at him, disgruntled that he'd jostled her. His gaze was even when he looked back. "What do you want me to do? They're not a danger to you."

She narrowed her eyes at him. "No, but I might end up being a danger for you if you don't find a way to get me out of this."

"This?" He narrowed his eyes at her and tilted his head to the press of organza and rhinestones around them. "I thought you liked what you did. Working with the girls-"

"Working with them, sure! Having them gush on me? Not exactly." She gave a visible shudder and felt his hand gather her closer. "I'm not… comfortable with that."

One of the girls touched her arm and then darted away giggling with some of her friends. Sloane squeezed her eyes closed and kept her lips pressed lightly together.

When she heard Vicente's voice whisper past her ear she shivered. "You really don't like the attention, do you?"

She shook her head, still blind to the wild colors swirling around her. "I just… It's just something I do to help."

"What if I could do something to make you forget that you're the center of attention?"

"I doubt you could but go ahead and give it a try."

He gave her a knowing smile. "Give me a second."

Her eyes flew open and fixed on him as he began to pull away.

Vicente looked down and she followed his gaze. Saw her hand on his arm, her white-knuckled hold. Gasping, she started to pull away, but he put his hand over hers instead.

When she met his eyes, she saw the glint of humor in them. "I'll be right back. Don't go anywhere."

She gave him a stare and a single raised brow to go with it. "I can't move."

The press of bodies wasn't going to let up anytime soon. If she were to guess, she'd say the entire neighborhood was there along with Vicente's family. So, there she stood as he waded two steps back into the fray and waved Blanca over.

The beautiful young woman reached out her arms and let her uncle tug her closer. When he leaned down to whisper in her ear she leaned in too. And after a few hushed words she turned ever so slightly to look over at Sloane.

Her chest tightened a bit as Blanca's lips curved into a smile, her eyes glittering with humor just like her uncle's had a moment before.

Blanca nodded.

Vincente leaned back from his niece and brought his hand up to his mouth.

Sloane felt her stomach turn over. "What is he-"

A whistle cut through the din and everyone turned in his direction.

Blanca waved her hands to the crowd and then cupped her hands around her mouth and yelled something in the other direction, toward the end of the basketball court.

Moments later music started up and the crowd on the court shifted, opening up space to dance. Sloane looked at the crowd as it moved away and then turned her eyes toward the only person moving in her direction.

There was a subtle rhythm to his movement, following the gentle bounce of the music.

Sloane knew that people were still watching her, but she couldn't seem to care, not when Vicente was watching her too. Only his eyes weren't full of curiosity or humor.

No, Vicente's eyes were dark and full of intent.

Bless her, but she didn't know what his intent was… and she couldn't seem to care.

Even when he was right in front of her, he wasn't still. His subtle movements, coupled with the rocking bounce of the music, made her feel like she was standing hip deep in the ocean and the shift of the currents were easing the stress away from her body.

"*Quiero bailar contigo.*" He broadened his smile. "Dance with me, Sloane."

Sloane blew out a soft breath and felt the rhythm of the music tug at her, almost as much as the look in his eyes.

It might have been her imagination but rationalizing it didn't do a thing for her heart… or other sensitive parts of her. The music, the look in his eyes, the slow, sly curve of his lips.

Conscious, clear thought?

Her instincts pushed away her conscience.

Her longing… her need… rushed to the surface when he held out his hands.

And she took them.

She took his hands and he pulled her closer.

CHAPTER 7

The cumbia rhythm rolled through his body, rocked him slightly back and forth, changed the pulse of blood through his veins. He watched Sloane and knew that the music touched her as well.

Honestly, he didn't know if she had any connection to the music or his culture, but as he felt the subtle tug on his hand and saw the gentle sway of her hips in time to the music, he felt himself drawn even closer to her and it wasn't about their physical proximity.

Her connection to him went deeper than the touch of her hand, or the scent of her perfume in his lungs.

It was easy to brush it away when they weren't touching, but here on the nearly empty dancefloor, when she held his hands, let him draw her closer, lean into the long line of his body with her curves, he was only too aware of how deep it went.

Leaning forward she gave him a pointed look. "I don't know how to dance to this."

His smile felt good. Free. Easy. Completely unlike himself

with someone outside of his family. "You might not know the steps, but you move to the music."

"Oh, good," she gave him a slight roll of her eyes, "I'm naturally inept."

"I didn't say that." Tugging on one of her hands, he let go of her other and stepped back.

Sloane stepped back shifting her balance to her back foot, only to have him tug her back. She moved closer and ended up pressed against him from her knees to her chest. A soft gasp of surprise was her only response.

He set his free hand on her lower back, holding her against him, and gave her joined hand a gentle nudge as he started to turn.

She followed effortlessly and it had nothing to do with skill on her part. He just made it so easy. Moving with him across the floor, rocking her hips with the slightest nudge from the hand he laid against her back, a little here… a little there… they moved together.

❧

He gave her a solid wall to lean on and she gave him her soft laughter and a gentle smile that grew along with her confidence as he led her through the steps.

A slight dip in the music moved through her body like a rolling stretch, brushing her body against his in all the right places. It hit him deep in his chest where his world had been silent much too long and all along his skin, making sure he was wide awake with this woman in his arms.

Her breath caught in her throat when she looked up into his eyes. It had to be the lighting, he decided, the lanterns, the soft, fading park lights that gave her soft green eyes a deeper cast.

"You're really good at this."

Vicente heard her voice, but he couldn't quite speak, not when he was barely able to catch his own breath.

"Do you," she continued to speak, and he was only too happy to let her as she moved against him in the same repetitive rhythm, making every inch of his skin tingle with awareness, "do you dance a lot?"

He took a step to the side and drew her along with him, making a half turn in the growing crowd. She followed, and the hem of her dress flared gently lashing at his legs through his pressed slacks. The touch was enough to draw him closer, pulling her against him.

There wasn't much room to maneuver with their bodies that close, but that only made things a little more interesting. He drew their joined hands to his waist and when he unwound his fingers from hers, he felt her set her hand on his waist, grip his side with a little squeeze.

He had a hand on her lower back, using his fingers to tilt her hips into his as his thigh slipped between hers.

If there had been more light, he would have looked down between them and seen the folds of fabric where her skirt rode up on his leg, but even with the low lights, he felt the heat of her thighs around his and heard the softest gasp of her breath as he pulled her close enough that she was nearly on the tips of her toes.

She gripped his shoulder with one hand and turned her head until their cheeks brushed lightly against each other. He wondered if she could hear his soft groan as her hair traced over his cheek, or maybe... yes, he felt her squeeze her thighs around his, rocking her heat against him.

Flicking his gaze up to meet hers he found her dark gaze fixed on him, her lips parted enough that he could see the hint of her pale white teeth between them.

He wanted to taste them, feel the scrape of her teeth

against his tongue, his neck, so many inches of his skin. He was a glutton for pain it seemed, especially if the source was Sloane King.

Vicente leaned closer, eager to whisper something in her ear and felt a sharp nip of pain on his earlobe.

Sloane… and those teeth.

He shifted his hips and heard the catch in her breath as she felt him press against her tender belly, hard and insistent. Needy and ready.

But was she?

Vincente reached a hand around her, to turn them both and felt the cell phone in his back pocket vibrate.

His movements stilled, and he heard Sloane's disappointed sigh.

"What happened?"

Vicente wrapped a protective arm around her and they walked to the edge of the dance floor before he unlocked his phone and listened to the voice message.

He met her eyes and saw the worry in them, but he knew he wasn't going to be able to make this easy on her. He wasn't going to be able to soften the blow.

Once the message ended, he typed out a quick text to let Travis know they were going to be on their way and then dropped his phone back in his pocket.

"What?" He heard the less than subtle worry in her tone. "What happened?"

"One of your distribution centers just burned down." His hand dug deeper into her side, keeping her on her feet. "I'm going to get my car and we're going to go over there and see what happened. Okay?"

He watched her falter, stumble to the side as if the ground beneath her feet had suddenly moved.

"Hey, I've got you."

She nodded, but he wasn't sure she actually heard him,

she was paler than usual, her face passive, but her body quivered against him. If he was any judge of women's moods, she was in shock and he needed to get her off her feet.

"Come on, sweetheart, let's get you off your feet."

As they started to walk, she swung her attention toward him. "I need to see what happened."

He nodded, unwilling to remind her that he'd already told her he was taking her to the site. "Sure, Sloane. I'll take you there."

She nodded, following along meekly beside him. "Good. I need to know what happened. I need to know."

When they reached the curb, his nephews started over in their direction. As he explained what he needed, he felt something touch his arm.

Sloane's hand traced down his arm to take his hand in hers, lacing their fingers together.

He tightened his fingers around hers and tugged her closer until she laid her cheek on his shoulder with a soft, plaintive sigh.

"Don't worry," he told her, "we'll figure this out, Sloane. We'll stop these people somehow."

Vicente said the words to comfort her, but he was beginning to wonder if he was telling her the truth. He really had no control over discovering the identities of the men who were destroying her work, but he did know one thing for certain.

If these people came after her, he'd put himself between her and danger in a heartbeat.

And it had nothing whatsoever to do with his job.

Not anymore.

It had everything to do with the woman at his side.

Sloane had a headache but there wasn't time to worry about it. Helping Hearts and Hangers was a charred mess, illuminated by a half dozen flood lights and the headlights of fire engines, and police vehicles. Engine 24 was finally packing up their hoses and Sloane was trying to give everyone their space. It made it easier on her head and her ears.

It was somewhere in the wee hours of the morning and she would likely be freezing if it wasn't for Vicente who had offered her a hoodie sweatshirt that he'd left in the back seat of his car. The garment fairly swam around her, but she didn't care much for the state of her own clothing when she was staring at the ruined mess of one of her oldest facilities.

Mentally she was calculating the amount of time it would take to rebuild the inside of the distribution center, and while that was happening, how they were going to service the members of this community while they waited.

She was trying desperately to ignore the pain in the center of her chest as she focused on the future, the next few steps she'd take after this was over.

Two police officers passed by talking to each other about the fire. She heard some of their words but not the entire conversation. No signs of gang activity. No signs of robbery. They were waiting on the Arson Investigator to go in once the Battalion Chief had declared the site completely out and safe, but they were fairly sure there wasn't going to be any kind of evidence left behind. It was the lack of evidence that had both men positing that it was arson. And that it was a professional behind the crime.

Sloane didn't care who was responsible at that point, she just wanted it to stop. All the good that she had been struggling to do. All the people she was trying to help. It wasn't going to make a difference if someone was trying to destroy it all.

"Such a waste," the words were cold and bitter on her tongue, but the ache and anger that was building inside of her seared her with pain. "Why would anyone do this?"

"Hey, babe, are you okay?"

Sloane heard the familiar voice of her friend and turned to see Hildie slam the door of her Mini Cooper and pick her way through the debris on the wet ground.

"Do you even have any idea how many uniformed officers that I had to flirt with or threaten to get them to allow me past the blockade?"

Even with all her anger and anxiety, it never failed to lift her spirits when she saw Hildie being, well, Hildie.

Sloane saw a subtle shift in the traffic pattern around the area. "About the same number of times you've had to make up crazy stories to distract me from my moods. I guess they have to start letting traffic through now that the fire is out."

"It makes sense," she sighed, "but there aren't that many cars waiting at this ungodly hour, and all people are going to do is drive through this muck and splash it all over the place."

Sloane tried to gesture to her friend and give her an alternate way to move through the soggy bog of water and debris from the clothing distribution center she'd opened nearly three years before. "Life has to move on, right?"

"Look at all this mess!" Hildie half-skipped, half-jumped over a standing puddle and managed not to splash any of the ash-laden water over her shoes. "This is crazy!"

It took an incredible effort to lock eyes with her friend. If anyone could read her moods, it would be Hildie. And Hildie didn't pull her punches. Not when it came to friends. Not when it came to Helping Hearts which they had built together over the last several years. It helped that all the floodlights were pointed away from her and the streetlights didn't offer much illumination in early morning hours.

Hildie touched her shoulder and waited until Sloane turned to look at her. "What's wrong?"

Shaking her head, Sloane let out a long breath and drew another one into her lungs. She knew how unsteady she was. She knew how much pain was surging through her veins. "Do you think this is because of me?"

Hildie stopped moving and took Sloane's shoulders in her hands. "Hey," she gave her friend a little shake, "don't even go there."

"How can I not? All this press? Don't think I haven't heard about the *#poorlittlerichgirl* online."

Hildie's brow furrowed. "Don't tell me you believe that."

"I don't," Sloane knew she didn't sound convinced, "but people wouldn't be saying it if they weren't thinking it."

"They don't know you, Sloane. They have no idea how much this hurts you. How much you care."

"It's not about the people who talk behind my back, not really. It's about the people who counted on the store. They're the ones who are going to suffer the most. What happens when someone needs clothes for their children and has to decide what's more important, groceries or clothes?"

Hildie gave her an encouraging smile. "We have food-banks in the area and-"

"Is that what's going to be targeted next?" Sloane heard her voice rising, felt the thinning of the space in her throat, and struggled to take a full breath. "Are they going to ruin perfectly good food to make a point?"

Hildie's fingers dug into her arms. "Stop this, Sloane. Stop."

"And if I'm the point, maybe I should just take a step back."

"No," Hildie's voice was rough, tight, "you're talking nonsense."

"I'm talking good sense, Hildie. If this is about me, the worst thing I can do is business as usual."

Sloane reached into her purse and dug out her phone.

She heard Hildie's quick indrawn breath and then her softly spoken question. "What are you doing?"

Ignoring Hildie for a moment, she turned on the phone and hit the speed dial.

"Sloane?" Hildie's voice had a panicked note to it. "What are you doing?"

Sloane saw her friend reaching out to take her phone, so she stepped back and put the phone up to her ear, walking away from the burn site toward the sidewalk closer to the traffic. "Yes, I'd like to speak to Glen McKinnon, please."

Hildie caught up with her, tugging on her arm. "Don't."

"Yes, I know he's sleeping. This is important," Sloane gave Hildie a pointed look. "Yes, I'll hold."

Digging in her heels, Hildie struggled to pull Sloane's arm away from her ear, but it wasn't working, Sloane wasn't giving an inch.

"You're not going to give this up, are you?"

Sloane didn't move, but she answered anyway, waiting on hold. "I'm giving it to you, Hildie. You're a dynamo and you practically own half my brain. You can do this, Hildie. People love you. My problems don't have to rub off on Helping Hearts. And I won't let my bad luck ruin everything good that I've done."

The hold music ended, and Sloane moved away from Hildie, turning her back to her friend. The slight would get her in trouble later, but Sloane knew that Hildie would understand in time.

"McKinnon here. This better be worth my time."

"Hey, Uncle Glen."

Silence, a heartbeat or two of silence. "What is it, Sloane? You do know what time it is?"

She felt the slightest twinge in her chest. It was just Uncle Glen. Sure he wasn't related by blood, but her parents had always considered her family and even though she was used to him being gruff and borderline insulting, but it didn't hurt any less. "The paperwork you wanted me to sign earlier this year?"

"Yes?" There it was, a happy tone that had nothing to do with her and only with how much he wanted his own way.

"I'm ready to talk about it."

She thought she heard a soft laugh on the other end of the phone, a self-satisfied chuckle. Still, she knew she was doing the right thing, even though it felt like her insides were being torn apart. "When can you get to my offices?"

"I thought you had to sleep?" She heard the cutting edge in her tone but couldn't stop herself.

"I admit that I'm tired of your petulance, but if you've finally seen the merit of my idea, then I have time to let you make amends, Sloane."

"Why does this have to be about you?" She squeezed her eyes shut. "Don't you understand how much this hurts? I built this foundation from the ground up. Everything we've done has been a labor of love."

Now he didn't bother to hide his laughter. "You're losing a series of flop houses and second-hand stores. You think you're being altruistic when you're just a bleeding heart, Sloane. People that don't deserve what you give them. And what do you get from it? A handful of humanitarian awards? Your father knew what was important. Your mother supported him. And you? What have you done? Go on some kind of religious mission to succor the downtrodden like some New Age Messiah if you want to feel good about yourself-"

"Can we not make this personal?"

"You're the one making it personal. Don't make me wait."

Sloane lowered the phone after he ended the call, staring at the phone as if she could bore a hole right through the phone with her eyes.

She expected to hear Hildie in her ear arguing with her, but when she realized that Hildie wasn't standing beside her a few feet away at the edge of the first responders, gesticulating wildly at Agent Bravo.

Hildie didn't look happy. Not one bit.

But Vicente? There was no way for her to see his reaction. The area behind him was dark, but there wasn't a lot of illumination in front of him either. What she could see gave him hard lines of exhaustion on his face.

Since the moment that they had arrived on site, he'd been in the thick of it, even at the edges of the scene, gleaning whatever information they could provide and passing it on to her.

They were all exhausted and Sloane knew she should be doing something. Thanking people, or making calls, but she didn't trust herself not to start crying and making things worse for everyone as they did their jobs. She always tried to be strong, the shoulder to lean on, the helping hand, but just this once. Just this one time when everything was so close to the edge she needed to stand by and hold herself together. That's all she had left.

Closing her eyes against the building migraine in her head, Sloane drew in a long steadying breath before letting it out.

She repeated the simple action again and again, struggling to tamp down on the building tide of anxiety inside of her. Her hand reached for her purse, only to realize she'd left it in Vicente's car.

It was sheer stupidity on her part. She should have

grabbed it when she got out of the car, but the columns of smoke… the flames eating their way through the structure had drawn her out of the car and into the thick rush of emergency personnel.

Now, as all the adrenaline started to bleed out of her veins she could feel her energy and her control flagging. As long as she could keep herself together, and hold all the panic inside, she had a hope of remaining on her feet so she couldn't embarrass the organization and all the people she hoped would come back to them after they cleaned up and rebuilt.

"Sloane!"

She heard her name as if someone was calling to her from a great distance, but she didn't want to answer them and she didn't want to look. All she wanted to do was have a few minutes to wallow in self-pity.

Didn't the world owe her that much?

Didn't she deserve a few minutes to be a sloth instead of the self-motivated woman she always presented to the world?

"Sloane, for the love of God-"

She lifted her head, intending to give Vicente Bravo a piece of her mind, but a blur of motion from the opposite direction pulled her attention.

It was still dark and that was probably why no one noticed it until it was close enough to cause such worry, but when she saw it-

Saw the low car with the wide base.

No lights.

Dark tinted windshield.

Too dark to see who was behind the steering wheel.

That's when panic set in.

And all the stupid, idiotic things she'd muttered in her head moments before seemed even more ridiculous.

Because she was about to die.

And boy, wouldn't that be the perfect way to end things.

She had time, she knew, to go one way or another, ducking away, but if she chose the wrong one...

"Sloane, here!"

She reached for him, giving into trust.

Giving into hope.

And a moment before the car bumped over the curb and missed her by the barest of margins, Vicente Bravo lifted her into his arms and pulled her to safety.

CHAPTER 8

Instinct told him to protect. Everything else told him he was going to be too late, but it didn't stop him. Instead, he pushed harder, and when he got his arms around Sloane he knew he'd have to work to let her go ever again.

The car careened into a newspaper box down the sidewalk, and even in the dark, Vicente could see papers spilling onto the pavement.

He saw the low-set frame and heard the ear-splitting scrape of metal on the curb as it dropped back to the road on the far side of one of the fire engines.

Uniformed officers ran after the car, but Vicente wasn't moving. Not while his heart had just begun beating again.

The thought that reverberated through his head was a simple yet damning mantra.

Just another inch. Just another second. She would be dead.

The words pounded through his skull as he held Sloane in his desperate embrace. He had almost made the worst mistake of his life.

"What," he felt, rather than heard the question that fell from her lips, "what happened?"

He wanted to keep her safely in his arms, but he knew he had to check her for injuries. With adrenaline rushing through both of them, there was no better way to make sure she was still in one beautiful piece.

So, he kept one hand on her at all times. Turning her slowly in one direction as his eyes and his other hand searched Sloane up and down for any sign of injury.

Finding none, he looked up at her as the EMTs tried to draw her over to the rig.

"No." He kept his hand on her, stepping closer to put her flush against his side and protectively tucked into his larger frame. "She stays with me."

One of the EMTs, a no-nonsense woman with a shrewd look in her eye and an apparently low bullshit meter gave him a look that would have made him think twice… if Sloane was any other person.

His thoughts didn't betray him as much as put things in startling clarity.

"Sir, we need to examine her."

He wanted to argue, but he took one more look at Sloane and saw the pale cast of her complexion, the grey undertones of her skin.

And then he felt her nails digging into his side, through his shirt.

She wore her nails short, ready for any kind of labor. Feeling their bite into his flesh, he knew he'd made a mistake.

"Sloane," he turned, trying to edge her toward the EMT, "let's go to the ambulance-"

"The car didn't touch me." She shook her head. Adamant. "No. I want to go home."

"Miss King," The male half of the pair cleared his throat and caught Sloane's attention, "we need to check and make sure you weren't hurt."

She turned back to Vicente and he felt her eyes on him like a physical weight. "I'm not hurt. I just want to go home. I'm exhausted. I promise... the car didn't touch me."

He was in between a rock and a cliff. Neither one offered much of a chance to make this better for Sloane.

He saw her lower lip tremble and lost the battle of indecision. Being back in the hospital and under the overly-watchful eye of the staff wouldn't help Sloane. Not then.

"I'm taking her home. If we find she needs medical attention later, I'll bring her in. But right now, she's still under protective custody."

"Miss King will have to sign saying she refused treat-"

"Where's the paper?" Sloane had found her balance and more of her voice. She gave the female EMT a look that didn't invite an argument, Sloane held out her hand. "I'd like to get home. We have a busy day tomorrow figuring out what to do about clean up."

They took care of the paperwork in moments, but it wasn't until Vicente had started up his car that Sloane spoke again.

"I should apologize to her," she began, "I'm sure I was a little short with her." She sagged against the seat in his car. "I didn't mean it like that. I was just so afraid I'd fall apart that the only way to hold myself together was..."

Sloane's voice faded off and Vicente wondered if she'd fallen asleep.

"I'm just not cut out for this." Her words were pitying, they were disappointed. "I thought I was stronger than this. That having a purpose would give me the will and the backbone to keep things on track.

"Now, I'm just worrying that by the time I extricate myself from the foundation, that there'll be something left to save."

"Hey," the pain in her voice hurt more than the heavy weight in his chest, "this isn't the end of anything. You've done amazing work building the foundation to where it is. This is just a setback, Sloane.

"Give yourself some time to digest it all. A day or two to breathe before you make a decision that you'll regret."

"This has been a long time coming," her words sounded like a confession, "I should have turned it over years ago, but I'm just too stubborn."

Everything about her words struck him like an off-centered punch. Not strong enough to knock him down, but enough to stagger him.

She'd said the words, but they didn't sound like her.

Didn't seem like her.

"Who told you that?"

Her lips parted and closed a moment later. She wasn't ready to say what was on her mind, but there was time.

Vicente's first duty was to get her home and safely inside. Hindsight being what it was, he had to acknowledge that she would have been better off at home when he went to the fire, but she'd insisted and he'd given in, using proximity as an excuse.

He was going to try to make up for it now.

Looking over at her for a precious second, he saw the downturn of her mouth and the slump of her shoulders. "Don't let people stop you from doing what you want to do. For years people tried to make me give up on applying to the FBI for a number of reasons, but what it really came down to was the fact that what I was doing made them uncomfortable. My dreams were bigger than theirs.

"If I had let them win. If I had listened to all the reasons why I shouldn't go after the goals I wanted, I don't know what I would be doing today, but I know one thing about you, Sloane."

A long moment passed between them before he heard her voice. "What's that?"

"You live for this foundation. It breathes with you, and its heartbeat is yours. The giving spirit that has made such a difference in this town is yours."

"Well," she shifted on the seat, "this spirit is tired. I don't know if I could survive it if even one more person was hurt because of me. All these women and their children already live with pain, suffering, and some with a target on their backs. If I added one more painful experience to their lives..."

He heard her drawn in a breath and then slowly let it go.

"Let it go for tonight, Sloane." He felt the weary pain in her body as if it was inside himself as well. "Take a few hours for yourself and when you've had time to really think about it, then you can make a decision for the right reasons and not a knee jerk reaction."

She didn't answer him, but he had a feeling that he'd made his point and she'd listened. From there, it was all up to her.

When they returned to her building, additional security was in place. This time it was a pair of FBI Agents watching over the building. Agent Mumford at the security desk alongside the regular security officer, and in the hallway outside of Sloane's door was Agent Hamada. She gave Vicente a quick rundown of the schedule and then stepped back to let Sloane and Vicente inside.

He didn't even bother to set his keys down on the counter, he just dropped them in his pocket and followed Sloane to her bedroom.

Vicente wasn't sure what he was going to do or say, but if there was some way he could offer her comfort, he was going to do it.

He'd never created something as big or important as the

storefront that had burned down, but he'd seen things he created, destroyed.

It was bad enough when you knew it was coming. Blindsided would leave the strongest person shaken, and he might not know exactly how Sloane was feeling, but he knew shock when he saw it.

And knowing that Sloane was suffering, hurt him more than he was willing to admit out-loud.

As soon as she was in her bedroom she headed straight for the bed and started to climb up onto it.

"Sloane?"

She paused, one knee on the mattress, the other leg still on the floor. "Yeah?"

"You want me to find something for you to change into? You're still wearing the dress from the party."

Her head dipped, and a laugh fell from her lips.

"That seemed like a lifetime ago… at least for me."

He wanted to hold her. Press her tightly to his body and let her know that he was there.

It was insanity, but it didn't seem to matter.

"Sloane, please," when he swallowed, all he felt was a raw pain in his throat. "What can I do to help you?"

She set both feet back down on the floor and turned to look at him. Her makeup was smudged around her eyes, her hair lopsided and ready to fall around her shoulders. Her dress was twisted and wrinkled around her body, but she was still the most beautiful woman he'd ever seen, because even with her life in turmoil, there was still a determined spark in her eyes.

She held out her hand to him and drew in a steadying breath. "Stay with me, Vicente."

He heard the words and prayed she didn't take them back. Not now.

"Sleep beside me. I don't think I can let you walk out the

door." She gasped in a breath. "I wasn't going to ask," she told him, "but I'm afraid that if I go to sleep by myself, with nothing to hold on to, that I'm going to disappear into the dark." The look in her eyes nearly slayed him. She looked so earnest he knew what he had to do.

The only thing his heart would allow him to do.

He managed to toe-off his shoes before he got to her side, but he had a feeling she wouldn't care. At least not this once.

Climbing up onto the bed, following in her wake, Vicente found what was likely the middle of the bed and laid down, opening his arms to her before he was settled.

And Sloane didn't argue or deny him.

She fit herself against the side of his body and laid her cheek on his shoulder, falling asleep as Vicente traced his fingers from her shoulder to the base of her neck and back again and again.

"Vicente?"

He heard her mumble, nearly sleep, most likely worrying again about something she could fix, at least not at that moment.

"Sleep, Sloane. Everything will be there tomorrow."

❧

And he was right.

When she awoke in the morning, a gasp on her lips and a missing beat in the rhythm of her heart, she felt his arms around her and settled back against his side.

A quick look told her that they probably hadn't moved an inch during the night. They were both still wearing the same clothes they had at the party and with the slightest movement of her hand, she felt the reassuring pulse of his heartbeat a few inches below.

Sighing softly, she melted back against the bed.

"You okay?"

Sloane turned her head and managed to tilt it up enough to see his face.

Vicente was wide awake beside her, his eyes searching hers.

"I want to say I am," she licked at her lips to ease the dry pull of her skin, "but I really don't know."

His smile was a slow curve of his lips and she felt parts of her body begin to wake up. Long forgotten sensations that she had been sure she'd never feel before she met this man, were now just within reach.

"What can I do?"

She felt him move his hand on her shoulder in a gentle comforting sweep over her bare skin.

So many words formed in her head. So many seemingly ridiculous things that she'd hate herself for saying.

But they all revolved around one thing. Touch.

There were very few people that Sloane touched by choice. That didn't apply to her work with the foundation. There she was used to holding hands or giving someone a comforting hug.

But allowing someone inside her heart where a touch could mean… and should mean so much more was something she didn't do often. Or hardly.

Hildie was the only one she cared deeply enough for as a friend to allow her close enough, but a man? She'd tried before. Almost engaged herself to someone before she realized that she'd never allow him in to see her shattered heart.

But Vicente…

Heaven help her, she wanted his touch. She wanted his arms around her. Wanted his hands on her skin.

Wanted him so far inside her that she'd always feel him there.

So she wouldn't ever be so alone again.

"Sloane?"

She felt him shift on the bed and looked to see that he was on his side, searching her face with his curious gaze.

"I'm sorry," the apology was as nature as breathing, "I was thinking."

"You were agonizing over something, baby. Do you ever give yourself a break?"

She shook her head. "It's hard to do that when I'm constantly worried about how I'm going to mess everything up. When I'm going to do something even more stupid than the last time. When I'm going to-"

"Don't do that to yourself. I'm supposed to keep you from being hurt. I'm not going to let you hurt yourself like this."

She felt his warm fingers on her jaw, holding her still under his gaze, but it didn't hurt. She felt comforted. She felt cherished.

And all of that, made her ache.

In so many delicious places.

"I think like this all the time," she shrugged a little, "when it's true, it's true. Everything I care about, everyone I love, gets messed up because of me at some point. It's better just to admit to it. Say it out loud. Remind myself so I don't make a mistake and let someone in just to ruin-"

He moved so fast that she didn't have time to realize what he'd done until it was over.

She was under him, pressed deep into her bed by his weight, her thighs cradling one of his legs between them, his fingers drawing her chin down as he swallowed her words and filled her mouth with his tongue.

The aches she'd felt had become fire. Flames licking at her skin with the same intensity that Vicente Bravo was sliding his tongue over hers.

She should tell him to stop.

Tell him that she'd just pull him down with her, no matter

how strong he was, but the things he was doing to her with just his mouth on hers made her shudder underneath him and her hands… they reached for him, needing him closer.

When her hands clutched at his shoulders, he moved his mouth from hers and she pulled him closer. "Don't," she begged, "don't stop."

The cheek he brushed against hers was slightly rough, but it only made the flames she felt lick at her skin, sending her a little closer to the edge.

She felt his fingers dig into her hip and she pressed closer, her leg hooking over the back of his.

His lips found her neck, placing a line of kisses along the side, making his way to her shoulder.

Her nipples tightened, and she arched her back searching for the hard wall of his chest. And when she found it, she felt his teeth on her skin. He mumbled something against her skin and it didn't matter that she couldn't hear the words, she felt them and the strong stroke of his fingers as they sought her thigh and pulled it tight against his hip.

All she wanted to do was hold him tight and not let go. Special Agent Vicente Bravo had managed to sneak past all of her walls and defenses and-

Someone was pounding on the door.

And there was shouting.

Sloane sat up as Vicente slid from the bed, clutching at her dress which was hanging onto her breast by a prayer. "What's going on?"

"That," he growled, with his head turned toward the open bedroom doorway, "is what I'm going to find out."

As she scooted to the edge of her bed she saw him reach for the nightstand and pick up his gun. It was a momentary shock, but she realized that the night before… or rather just a few hours before when they'd fallen into bed, she hadn't spared a moment to wonder where he'd put his gun.

She got to her feet and tried to set her dress back into place, but something was twisted and made it difficult to fix it. Sloane followed Vicente into the main room of her apartment and then backed up a few steps when he waved her behind the corner.

CHAPTER 9

Vicente could hear three voices outside. Point of fact, he was sure the entire building could hear the three voices outside. He was sure they'd have a noise complaint on their hands.

"Sir, please sir, you have to step back!"

Agent Hamada was trying to diffuse the situation, but-

"You don't tell me what to do, young lady!"

A gasp from the hall turned his head.

"That's my uncle."

Vicente swore under his breath. Glen McKinnon wasn't someone you wanted to tangle with about anything. The man had demolished businesses that were bigger than small countries and then had a relaxing cigar and snifter as things burned to the ground.

A quick peek out of the corner of the shade told him there wasn't anyone else lurking outside and he disarmed the security and opened the door.

McKinnon's eyes locked on him the moment he did.

"You!"

Vicente stepped into the open doorway. "Agent Bravo. Is there something you need?"

"I need you to get out of my way or produce my niece, then feel free to make yourself scarce. I'll take care of everything from here."

"Sir," Vicente hated when people told him what to do, but when they were dismissive, it really twisted him up inside, "I'll have Sloane call you-"

"Sloane is it?" The man was tall, having a few inches on Vicente which wasn't easy, but he had worked hard on perfecting the kind of glare that made most people cower. On that, he had nothing on Vicente.

"Yes, Sloane. If you need to see her-"

Glen McKinnon moved through the FBI agents like a battleship in the ocean, nearly bowling them over.

Vicente didn't fault the agents, they couldn't justify knocking one of the most influential men in San Antonio on his ass. Add to that his relationship with Sloane and it made no sense to take him down himself.

Yet.

"Vicente?"

He heard Sloane's voice, but he also saw the narrowed eyes of her Uncle and the sardonic twist to his lips. The man probably didn't miss much.

"Go ahead and let him in. I was supposed to go to his office to see him this morning."

Now assured of his acceptance into the apartment, Glen stood up straight and turned to give the agents behind him a grin that would likely still be stuck in their craws for months to come as he stepped through the doorway and into Sloane's apartment.

"It's not like to you be late, Sloane."

Vicente had to give her credit. She didn't physically shrink from the older man's glare, but he could have sworn he saw a shadow of something in her eyes.

"I am sorry, Uncle Glen. There were some additional

trials last night."

"The near miss this morning, perhaps?"

Vicente focused more attention onto the older man.

Turning to look at Vicente, he nodded. "I have eyes and ears everywhere in San Antonio, Agent Bravo. Nothing happens in my town that I don't know about. Still, I'm unimpressed by the lack of respect your FBI office has shown me during this trying time. It's part of the reason I wanted Sloane to have protection from the local police. They understand who they're dealing with."

Sloane wrapped her robe around her body tighter. "I'm sorry I don't have coffee for you-"

"No sense in wasting time, my dear." Reaching into the sleek leather portfolio he'd brought with him, McKinnon withdrew a sheaf of papers that looked thick enough to be a textbook if it had been bound. "After our conversation, I took the liberty of drafting up some papers to transition your foundation into the McKinnon holdings. I can assure you I will have the best people assigned to your charity, and you'll have the peace of mind to sit back and relax. All this tension and your brushes with danger can't be good for your health. All you have to do is sign."

And damn if the man didn't set down a pearl inlaid Montblanc pen on top of the papers.

With that done he sat down on the couch and gestured for her to sit in the armchair beside him.

Sloane folded herself into the chair and reached for the papers.

As she leaned over. Vicente caught McKinnon glaring at her robe.

From where he was sitting, Vicente couldn't see much, but whatever the older man saw, he certainly didn't like. The garment covered her from her shoulders to her knees, held securely by a belt, it wasn't revealing anything in the slightest, but it seemed to aggravate McKinnon just the same.

Settling the papers in her lap, she poured over the first page, stopping a few times with a narrowed or questioning look. "I'm not sure we're on the same page about this." Lifting her head, her hair fell back from her face and Vicente could easily see the troubled look in her eyes. "I'm not interested in giving up the foundation to have it become a forgotten doll in the attic of your holdings. I have poured my heart and soul into this for years."

"And nearly beggared your family's holdings to do it."

Vicente didn't like the way he spoke to Sloane, but this wasn't his call as much as he wanted to interrupt.

"It's my inheritance. You told me it was mine to do with as I chose."

"Within reason," McKinnon clarified, "and with proper consideration given to my advice."

He saw the tick in the other man's jaw, saw the beads of sweat on the other man's forehead and the red flush on the back of his neck.

"I thought you'd put it into investments, drop a few thousand here or there on charities and live happily the rest of your life." Standing, McKinnon reached out and snatched the pen from Sloane's hand. "You're not the intelligent young woman your parents thought you were. I was still willing to give you the benefit of the doubt. Your father and I were as close as brothers, and I hate that he's gone, but if he knew what you were going to waste everything he worked so hard to give you..." McKinnon shoved his pen into his coat pocket and Vicente was worried that he would rip the pen straight through to the lining, but he figured the businessman could afford it. "He'd turn over in his grave."

With a glaring shake of his head, Glen McKinnon sent

one last parting shot at his niece. "When you've come to your senses, call me. Until then, I have business to do."

When the door swung shut on his exit, Vicente didn't follow him and set the alarm immediately. He took the other man's seat on the couch and leaned forward, bracing his forearms on his thighs.

Sloane was staring at the first page of the papers that her uncle brought her. He watched her eyes moving over and over from one side of the page to the other, and the more she did it, the more agitated she became.

"Sloane?"

She didn't react to his voice. She didn't seem to notice him sitting there.

"This isn't what I meant." She shook her head and her honeyed blonde hair shook and caught on her shoulders. "This isn't what I want."

He saw the dawning horror in her eyes as she read over the first page of the document again.

"He's going to destroy everything I've built. It'll be gone. Dismantled. He just doesn't understand."

She lowered her head and her hair covered her face like a curtain. He would have left her alone to think if it hadn't been for her leg. It was her knee he noticed first, bared from the hem of her robe it shook and the quiver continued down her calf.

"Sloane?"

He watched as she slowly curled in on herself, the papers falling from her hands onto the carpet around their feet.

"If I give up," he could barely hear her words, "then what am I going to do?"

Vicente moved to the edge of the couch until his knee was almost touching hers. "No one says you have to give up."

"He always said I was cursed."

A tear fell from behind her hair and fell onto the silk of her robe.

"That I'm the reason they all died."

"Hey," he leaned forward and took her hand in his, "don't do this to yourself."

"Why not?" She turned toward him and her hair fell back to reveal her red-rimmed eyes and tear-streaked cheeks. "It's true. My parents are dead. My sister died. And here I am."

He looked down for a moment when he felt several points of pain on the back of his hand. Sloane had covered their joined hands and her fingers were digging into his skin, making pale halos against his darker complexion.

Vicente met her eyes again and this time he wasn't going to let go, not when he saw the wild grief looking back at him.

"Here you are, Sloane. With me."

Her eyes widened and when they slowly narrowed to their normal size he saw the change in her.

Saw how her breathing changed ever so slightly, slowing, easing the jagged rise and fall of her shoulders from a few moments before. Her green eyes darkened as she looked at him, her gaze moving over his face, searching for something.

❧

"With you?" The words had a wistful tone to them, a soft breathy whisper in her own ears. "You mean you're here until they find out who is trying to destroy me… or I die. Then no one will *be* with me, Vicente. We all die alone." She swallowed at the knot in her throat, but it wouldn't go down. "And some of us die more alone than others."

"Sloane, stop."

She shut her eyes and opened them again. "You know, my uncle thinks he knows me. He thinks if he just waits long enough, pushes hard enough, I'll give up and sign those damn papers."

He didn't say anything back to her and she was grateful. She didn't think she could hear another nice, sympathetic word from Vicente Bravo.

"There's one thing he didn't count on, you know?"

Vicente swept his tongue over his bottom lip and she felt something spark inside of her, something lower... baser... to go along with the flare of outrage in her chest.

"He didn't count on how much of my parents I carry with me. I'm not just a King because I carry the name. Generations of Kings left their marks on Texas because they were just too damn stubborn to give up.

"Land disputes. Cattle rustlers. Envy. Murder. Sin and temptation have snapped limbs off the family tree more than any natural disaster could, but we're still here." She laughed and he heard the rough scratch of it in her throat. "And I'm going to be here for a long time if I have anything to say about it."

She saw a little bit of relief in his expression and it made her smile even more.

"You were worried that I was going to fold, right? You thought I was going to curl up in a little ball and cry all day?"

He didn't have to open his mouth to answer her, she saw it written in his eyes.

"Well, I'm not. I'm feeling like I want to flex a little of my own muscle today, Agent Bravo. I want to make my own decisions."

She watched him let out a slow breath as he leaned back against the sofa cushions.

He still wore his clothes from the night before, looking a bit rumpled like he was ready to do the walk of shame as he went home.

But he wasn't.

Going home, that is.

He was there.

With her.

And she wasn't going to waste any more time waiting to see what the *right* move was. She was done doing that.

She stood up, nudging the paperwork out of the way with her foot.

Sloane watched as Vicente pulled his legs back until his calves were up against the front of the sofa. He was expecting her to walk past him.

Well, she was done doing what was expected.

She stopped when her feet were tucked in between his, her eyes cast down at his face, her hands nervously smoothing her palms against her sides. The soft silk felt like heaven against her skin, but she was dying to know what his morning stubble would feel like as well.

And after that, she wanted more.

Leaning over, she set her hands on his shoulders and looked him square in the eye.

"This morning," she watched him carefully, "did you want me?"

She saw his eyes darken as he drew in a breath that filled his lungs.

"Vicente?"

His breath caught at the sound of his name on her tongue, and she rolled the sensation of it over and over in her mouth.

He watched her like a hawk, his gaze moving over her face and down to her throat before dipping to the fabric loosening at the neckline of her robe.

"I remember," she spoke again and watched him shift against the sofa, "I remember how hard you were, the way you moved against me."

"Yes," the words rolled off of his tongue like honey, thick and warm, "I wanted you."

She moved closer and he leaned his head back just enough to keep looking in her eyes. While she had him focused on her face she straddled him on the sofa, loving the soft brush of his slacks against the backs of her thighs.

By the time she settled herself on his lap, she felt the hard press of his erection between her thighs.

"Looks like you still do."

Gripping his shoulders in her hands she rolled her hips against him, sliding over his thick length with a soft sigh. She closed her eyes and repeated the motion again, concentrating her focus on the feel of their delicious friction.

When she opened her eyes, she saw the way his hands fisted the sofa cushions as if he needed help keeping his hands to himself.

"Are you trying to hold back on me, Vicente? Don't you want to touch me as much as I want to touch you?"

He bit his teeth into his bottom lip and narrowed his eyes as she eased her thighs apart, just the littlest bit, bringing her flush against him with a slow breathy sigh.

"That wasn't a no, Vicente."

"I should have kept my hands off of you this morning."

She shrugged and took her hands from his shoulders. Maybe it was her imagination, but she could have sworn she saw a flicker of disappointment on his face.

But she definitely saw a flare of interest when her hands tugged at the belt of her robe and let the ends fall from her hands.

And his gaze fell from her face to her bare breasts and it was easy to read the appreciation in his gaze and the warming flush under his darker complexion.

"Do you know what you're doing to me, Sloane? Do you have any idea what you're playing with here?"

She shook her head, but kept her eyes level, focused on him.

It was a heady sensation for her, knowing that she had him on edge. She'd closed herself off for so long that feeling the physical evidence of his arousal pushed tight between her legs felt as if she'd somehow conquered something from her past.

"I'm not playing with anything, Vicente. I'm not about games. Especially not with you." She rose up slightly on her knees and cupped his face in her hands.

Sloane leaned forward until she could feel his breath on her lips.

"Tell me, Vicente. Tell me if you want me, or am I making a fool of myself, asking you to touch me... taste me... make me fall apart like no one has ever done before.

"I want to lose myself in your arms and feel you deep inside of me." She hesitated, losing some of her confidence. "I've never asked a man to-"

He surged up against her, his hands grasping the sides of her face mirroring her own, sealing their lips against each other. She held on to him as his tongue traced the seam of her lips and she sighed when she opened her mouth and let him in.

Still, she wasn't going to let him take charge of all the fun. Pushing him back against the sofa, she used her hands to turn his head slightly to one side and traced her nose along the side of his neck just beneath his ear. She felt him shudder, just a little, as she drew in his scent.

It was that subtle spicy scent that she was desperate to taste, and so she did.

Parting her lips over his pulse, she swept her tongue over the same spot, listening to him mutter unintelligible words under his breath before she scraped her teeth along the same path.

His hands found their way back to her shoulders and slid the neckline of the robe down her arms to her elbows.

The shift of her clothing pulled her arms tight and she felt her elbows tuck in against her sides and lift her breasts just a little higher and into his hands.

How he found them with his face lifted up to the ceiling she didn't know, but she didn't really care when she felt his thumbs sweep over her nipples, catching ever so slightly on the tightened peaks.

Sloane's teeth bit deeper into his neck at her sudden jolt of pleasure at his touch.

Turning her head slightly to the side, she placed her cheek against his heated skin and moaned. "More."

Again, his thumbs danced over her nipples and she drew in a stuttering breath when his fingers pinched both of them, twisting ever so slightly as his pulled on her tender flesh.

He turned his head toward her as his fingers worked her flesh over again. "More? Is this what you like?"

She felt her body weep as his fingers tugged her closer to him, leaning forward when he cupped her breasts in his hands, using his palms to soothe the stinging sensations.

"Yes," she leaned into his touch, "I like your hands on me, Vicente, but-"

"You need more, don't you?"

"You can play with me later, Vicente. You can do whatever you like to me… later. Right now," she pushed her hands between them, her fingers tugging at his shirt front, plucking at his buttons in much the same way he'd touched her breasts, "I need you inside me."

"Sloane-"

"We can do slow later. I need you hard… and fast… and so damn deep I-"

He stood, wrapping one arm around her back, the other pushing off the sofa arm to get him onto his feet. She clung to him with an arm around his neck, her other hand working at the buttons down the front of his shirt.

"We could have stayed there," she slanted her lips across his mouth, "I wouldn't mind."

He chased her lips, searching for another kiss and she felt him reach a hand under her and hoped he was going for his belt. "I would mind, Sloane. The first time I take you I need room. I want you laid out on that bed of yours so you can watch everything I do to you."

Vicente stepped through the doorway into her bedroom and managed to lay her down and avoid her hands as she tried to pull him down with her.

He knelt on the bed and spread her robe open. "And here I thought you'd done all the work for me."

Sloane smoothed her hand down the side of her body and hooked her thumb into the waistband of her panties, sliding around to the narrow band high on her hip. "I was hoping you wouldn't mind offering me a hand."

He muttered something under his breath and she smiled at him. "You keep doing that," she smoothed her tongue over her lower lip, hungering for a taste, "talking to yourself when you look at me."

"I'm not talking to myself," he shook his head, "I'm praying for patience, Sloane."

"Patience?" She lowered her other hand and hooked her thumb on the opposite narrow band. "Am I that annoying?"

"No," he moved closer on his knees and then dropped down landing on his fists on both sides of her hips, his face less than a foot from her belly, "you're that tempting and I'm trying to hold back because I don't want to scare you."

She planted her feet on the bed. "Like I told you, we can do slow later, I need you." She lifted her bottom off the bed and started to push her panties down over her hips.

Before she got it down to her tailbone, he pulled the delicate garment from her fingers, and set a knee under her backside to keep her hips high enough to pull her panties free without making the motion uncomfortable for her.

For one tiny moment she thought of thanking him for the consideration, but then her focus was elsewhere.

With the heady sensation of her panties sliding over the backs of her thighs, she saw him reach for his belt with his free hand. The buckle was undone and all it took was a tug to free both ends.

She watched him make quick work of his top button and then slide the zipper pull down with a hushed whisper.

Sloane reached out a hand, eager to touch him, but he brushed it away.

"Stop distracting me!"

He pushed his pants down off so his hips and his boxers went with it.

When Sloane saw the crown of his cock revealed by the rush of movement, she felt her mouth go dry, and an answering rush of liquid heat between her thighs.

Vicente lifted up, his hands shoving his clothing down his thighs, baring himself to her gaze from the root of his cock to the top. "I've felt you in my dreams, Sloane. Held you in my arms. Taken you over the edge with my name on your lips."

She panted out a breath and then another. "Then why are you making me wait, '*Cente*? Take me there."

He lowered her down to the bed and pushed his pants to the floor, only sparing a moment to reach into his wallet for a silver packet.

She lowered her knees to the side, keeping her eyes on his face so she could see his reaction. Revealing herself before his watchful gaze was a leap of faith in and of itself.

He laid his hands on her calves, smoothing a heated trail along her skin, putting just enough pressure on the inside of her knees to press them down against the mattress.

Vicente crawled between her legs, balancing one hand on the sheets beside her while the other turned, and he traced his trimmed nails along the tender inside of her thigh.

Shifting on the bed beneath him, she tried to keep herself still before him, but couldn't seem to help the subtle lift of her hips from the cool bedding beneath her. "Come on-"

"I'm going to taste you, Sloane. Maybe not today, but soon. You can't show me-"

"Enough," she sat up and hooked a hand around the back of his neck, pulling him down for a kiss. Once she had her lips on his she wrapped her other arm around his shoulder and firmly planted her hand on his back.

She wasn't sure exactly what his reaction had been to her surprise attack, but it felt like just a few heartbeats before he hooked her leg over his forearm and slid the tip of his erection through her folds. A second heady swipe against her sex was all it took and when he shifted his hold on her, she sank down onto his cock, her whole body wrapping around his heat, embracing him as if her life depended on it.

And maybe it did.

The aching loneliness in her heart was gone, chased away like the dawn pushed back the night.

All it took was Vicente sinking into her willing heat, filling her up.

The groan that poured from her lips vibrated through her body and then his. He bit down on his bottom lip as his eyes raised to hers.

The dark passion in his gaze threatened to swallow her whole, and pull her under, but he held her up, gave her his air, and his body.

It was a heady combination that began to heat the air around them. The first thrust of his hips pushed the air from her lungs, the second pulled it back in. As he stroked into her body over and over all she could do was hold on and reach for that elusive edge, climbing higher and higher as he held her against him. The tight tips of her nipples drew long invisible lines up and down his chest as he thrust up into her body, pushing her up toward heights she'd never seen before… never felt.

And it was there, she couldn't see the edge, but she felt it.

And she felt his mouth feeding on hers.

And his hands everywhere on her skin.

Her back bowed and her hands clung to him even as everything she was imploded and reformed in his arms.

He didn't let her go. He didn't lay her down.

As he came with a shout, his body locked with hers, he gathered her closer and held her against his heat, blocking out the world.

CHAPTER 10

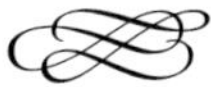

When the pounding started, Vicente thought it was in his head. The incessant rhythm could have been ignored if it hadn't turned into the 'shave and a haircut' riff that his family had used since his earliest memories and coupled with the 'Bidi Bidi Bom Bom' ringtone that identified the evildoer as his sister Pilar he knew he had better answer the phone before she knocked down the door.

"Why are you calling me?"

"Well, well, you were asleep."

The smug huff in her tone grated on his nerves.

"I was getting some rest. You might have heard that we were out in the early morning hours and-"

"*Hermano,* we were all out in the early morning hours. The *Quinceanera* finished just after midnight and the rest of the family stayed to do clean-up. So, let me in. I have coffee and food for lunch. We need a plan."

"We," he hissed through the phone, "aren't ready to deal with your kind of sunshine this early."

"Early," she drew the word out with a definite grin in her tone, "as in early afternoon? It's almost two, Agent Bravo, and you are asleep on the job." Her jab was punctuated with a laugh. "I'm sure Sloane is ready to kick you off of her couch, lazy boy."

Vicente looked over at the other side of the bed and resisted the urge to smile. Sloane was fast asleep, naked except for the sheet that one of them had managed to pull up before they fell asleep.

He could still feel her lips and hands all over his body, the slight rasp of her toes against his legs, the soft gasp when he'd closed his lips over her-

"Exactly what is taking you so long to come and open the door, *'Cente*? Her place isn't that big. Hell, it's almost the same size as mine, so why didn't she come to the door and-"

"Can you stop talking long enough for me to answer, *Chiquita*?" He grinned, knowing that calling her a little girl would buy him a moment of sisterly indignation. "Let me get some clothes on and I'll-"

As a police officer, Pilar had the same extensive vocabulary of curse words and chose that moment to display them in a vastly amusing chain of expletives before she hissed into the phone. "Then do it and open the door before I break it down, *cabrón*."

His mouth quirked up at the corner. "Keep your pants on, Pilar. I'll be right there."

"At least I have some on."

Ending the call, he set the phone down on the bed and easily found his pants at the floor by the foot of the bed. Shrugging them on, he didn't bother to look for his shirt. The color of the dress shirt blended in with some of the bedclothes and it wasn't worth letting his sister stew any longer.

Vicente walked into the main room of the apartment scrubbing his palm over his face, trying to dispel some of the remaining sleep from his eyes.

A quick tap at the security panel and the green light told him it was safe to open the door. A couple of deadbolt locks and a few seconds later and he pulled the door open.

Pilar pushed in, her knowing eyes seeking him out behind the door with an eagle-like glare. "Did you-"

He touched his finger to his mouth. "*Cállate*! Get inside before you start on me."

She pursed her lips together and pushed the door open further with her elbow, forcing him to catch it with a hand before the inside knob hit him in the crotch.

"Watch what you're doing."

Pilar arched a brow at him, her perfectly painted lips in a smirk as she looked him up and down. He knew what she was seeing and she didn't like it one bit. Still he shut the door and locked her *inside* the apartment with him.

His hair was mussed. His shirtless chest probably had a few well-placed bite marks if his memory served him correctly. And his pants.

He looked down to make a quick check and heard his sister groan.

"Thank goodness you managed to zip up before you came to the door."

"Can we get past this?"

Her eyes widened as she dropped her chin to stare back at him. "Past 'this'?" She gestured at his half-clothed body. "You mean to tell me that you slept with the woman you're protecting, and you think we're not going to talk about it?"

"Talking is one thing," he reached up a hand and pushed his fingers through his hair hoping to settle it down a bit. The thick strands curled if they weren't combed into place moments after waking up, he knew what he must look like. "I'm not ready for you to grill me, Pilar."

"You don't think this is a problem you need to deal with?"

He took the tray out of her hand and set it on the coffee

table and then took the paper bag from the crook of her arm and set it down too. Taking Pilar by the upper arms, he led her over to the sofa and set her down. Looking her straight in the eyes. "You need to leave this alone."

"She's your job, *'Cente*. She's your protective detail! What were you thinking?"

Vicente shook his head. "I'm not going to explain this to you, Pilar."

"Well you're going to have to explain it at some point, Vicente, because the two of you bleed chemistry all over each other. Someone's going to notice and it's going to be bad."

"I'd rather not think about bleeding." Sloane's voice reached him from the hallway and he had a moment to prepare himself before she stepped into view, her sable hair tumbled about her shoulders. She looked well and truly tumbled and the flush on her cheeks spoke volumes. "Pilar. I'm sorry, I didn't hear you come in."

Vicente turned to look at his sister and hopefully give her a look to convince her to leave it alone. After all, what she was feeling had to do with him, not Sloane.

Pulling free of his restraining hand, Pilar stood, with Vicente less than a second behind her. "Hey, Sloane, sorry to bother. I thought you two… I mean, I thought you'd be up for some company."

Brushing some of her hair back from her face, Sloane flickered a glance at him and he could tell she was worried.

Giving Pilar a pointed look, he walked toward Sloane. "Let's go and talk for a minute, Pilar can wait for us."

It killed him to see Sloane look as if she had done something wrong and was waiting to have Pilar rip into her the way her uncle had done just a few hours ago.

Sloane was an amazing woman, but she'd received too little support from her family.

When he reached her, he set his hand on the small of her

back, feeling the silk of her robe warm under his hand as he moved her back into the bedroom.

He knew how right he was about her worries when she stopped short as he closed the door.

Taking a step away from him, she smoothed her hands down over her robe. "Why is your sister here?"

He opened his mouth to answer and she rushed right on.

"Does she know?" Sloane looked up into his eyes and a moment later she flinched and shivered. "She does, doesn't she?"

She looked at him, noticing, perhaps for the first time that he was bare chested, and that made her eyes widen as her mouth dropped open.

"I can't believe this."

She must have been more than a little tired and confused, because a moment after she'd been upset about his sister learning that they'd been intimate with each other, she dropped her robe on the floor and walked across the hall and into her bathroom with a stack of clothes under her arm.

Needing to talk to her, Vicente followed Sloane in and closed the door behind him with a quiet but definite click of the lock. "It's going to be okay."

"I don't see how it's going to be okay." Shaking her head as she dropped her clothes on the closed toilet seat lid, Sloane swung open the door to her shower and reached in to turn on the water. The shower head erupted with a steady spray and using her bare wrist she tested the heat. "Your sister knows we slept together. I don't know how we're going to get past this. She's going to hate me.

"And I know how close your family is, so they're going to hate me. Not to mention that they'll never respect me after this." She turned to look at him and then turned away to step inside the shower. "And really, what does it matter. It's not like you're going to have anything to do with me after this... this job is over."

"Sloane-"

"I get it," she assured him as she picked up her bottle of body wash and splashed some of it on her scrub, "this morning was all kinds of nuts. We'd been to the party and then a crime scene. I blubbered all over you and then jumped on you like a crazy woman. Go ahead and put it all on me, Vicente. I can take it. I don't mind that she'll think I'm a-"

He pulled the shower door open and stepped inside with her.

The look on her face was simple to understand, but she said the words anyway. "You're insane!"

Vicente shrugged and pulled her closer, his hands on her hips. "You're gorgeous."

Her cheeks were nearly red, a combination of the heat in the shower and his touch. If she was anything like him she was remembering the feel of his hands on her hips the second time he'd brought her to orgasm underneath him. "You make me do crazy things, Vicente."

Ignoring her look of warning, he pulled her out from under the shower spray and flush against his body. He sealed her lips with a kiss before she could say a word, both soothing and inflaming her with his tongue dragging against hers. When he heard the soft slap of her scrub hitting the tiles at their feet he pulled back.

Her eyes lifted to see the thin rivulets of water coursing down his forehead and over his cheeks. "And maybe I make you do some crazy things too."

The smile he felt on his lips was as satisfying as it was easy, as if he'd worn it all his life. "I want you not to worry about Pilar. She's mad at me. She'll probably try to protect you from me and my wicked ways. So don't worry about her saying anything bad about you, she knows where the blame is going to sit. Firmly on my shoulders."

He leaned in closer when her body's tense posture eased a little and her breathing slowed into a gentle rhythm. Placing a soft kiss on her lips he gave her hips a little comforting squeeze. "Now, finish your shower. I'm going to change my clothes and then we're going to see what Pilar wants."

Stepping away, he nudged the door open with his elbow and watched her back up under the rush of water.

"I'd love to join you, but I think that would test my sister's patience too much, or she'd end up coming in here and kicking my ass for taking advantage of you."

He shook his head when she opened her mouth to argue with him.

"Don't worry. Just don't take too long or she'll think you're in here crying and then she'll really kill me."

When he shut the door to the bathroom and started to cross the hall, he caught a reflection of his sister's wide-eyed shock in a picture frame on the wall.

Giving her a half wave and a smile, he disappeared back into Sloane's bedroom to look for a change of clothes.

❧

When Sloane joined the Bravo siblings in her living room she paused just outside of the seating area, waiting as if she was worried that she'd overstep her bounds.

It was silly, she knew, but there was something odd going on between the siblings. She'd had the same uncomfortable energy between herself and Kimberly too many times to count.

And for that moment, as she hovered just outside their hushed conversation, Sloane wished that her sister was there to talk to, even if they would have devolved things into a heated argument, because at least that meant her sister was alive.

"Sloane?"

Shaking herself free of her reverie, she turned to look at Pilar. The younger woman's eyes were full of concern.

"Are you okay?"

"I'm fine." The words tumbled out right on time with her usual carefree shrug. "Thanks."

The two Bravo siblings shared a look and then Pilar moved over, patting the seat between her and Vicente. "Have a seat."

When Sloane didn't move she saw Pilar's expression soften as if it was a conscious effort to put her at ease.

It worked.

"I'm not going to bite."

More tension fell away from Sloane's shoulders and she offered the deputy a smile of her own.

"Besides," Pilar continued with the corners of her mouth turning up into little points, "I see you took a bite or two out of my brother before I got here."

Before Sloane could tense up, Vicente threw an accent pillow at his sister and Pilar managed to duck the fringed projectile without even looking to see where he'd aimed it.

Obviously brother and sister were old hats at pillow fighting, but she had a feeling they were hamming it up for her benefit. It brought a slight smile to her lips.

"Seriously, Sloane," Pilar gave the empty seat another pat, "I'm not going to jump on you or ask any specifics, because you and the Virgin Mary should know that I have no interest in learning about my brother's supposed prowess in bed. That," she said with assurance, "would make my therapist a rich woman… and then some."

"Well I know a thing or two about that." Skirting between

Pilar's knees and the coffee table, Sloane eased past the officer and sat on the empty cushion. "After my parents died, Kimberly and I had a couple of therapists each, and then when we lost Kimberly it seemed like I had a staff of them, all eager to help me work through the issue."

Vicente's hand was warm on her knee. "Did they help?"

"One, and I kept her after I realized that the others were just gathering information for a future 'tell all' book about the sad little heiress. I had other coping mechanisms that worked better than talking anyway, so I kept Dr. Chambers and spent the time and money that was going to the others to do some riding and of course, start my foundation." Sloane leaned on the back of the sofa and looked at Pilar, speaking as if they were old friends. "After a while the foundation consumed almost all of my time, but I've never looked back, not when I'm doing something that feels so good and means so much to the people we've helped over the years."

With a sigh, Sloane shook her head.

"I just hope we can get this over and done with so things can get back to normal. Our community outreach is suffering."

"That's why I'm here." Pilar shifted beside her, turning slightly so she could look Sloane in the eye. "I think what you said is true for most of us working on the case. We all feel like we're just waiting for something to happen.

"I came over today with some news." She gave her brother a pointed look. "We found one of the men who ran from the accident."

Sloane saw Vicente shift in his chair and pull out his phone, likely looking for a message or a text.

"I don't see anything."

"I told Cruz that I'd let you know."

He gave his sister a withering stare. "That's Special Agent Livingston to you, Deputy Bravo."

She waved off his order. "I've known him since before I had my first bra, he's Cruz when I'm not in uniform."

Sloane couldn't quite hide her smile at the antics of the siblings.

"Anyway," Pilar cleared her throat, "before I was so rudely interrupted by *Special Agent Bravo,* I was going to tell you both that when we found him he had a nasty infection. A cut he sustained in the crash was infected and by the time he went through the process of having the infected flesh excised and cleaned, he was put under to give his body a chance to fight off the infection."

"They should have called me in," Vicente's free hand was fisted in frustration and Sloane felt the hand he had on her go hot with his emotions. "What did the doctors say?"

Sloane moved her arm until she took his hand in hers.

He gave her a soft smile as his sister started to answer him.

"He should be awake in a few hours. If you want me to stay with Sloane while you go down to the hospital, I'm here."

Looking at Pilar, Sloane didn't see anything but an earnest offer of help and it went a long way to easing her worries.

Sloane turned her attention back to Vicente and saw the concern in his eyes. "I'm fine here. You go. You'll feel better if you're there for the questioning."

She saw his smile and she gave him one right back.

"I know I'll feel better if you're there."

He gave her hand a gentle squeeze, but a moment later, he turned to look at his sister. "Pilar?"

Sloane turned as well, splitting her attention between one sibling and then the other.

"Pilar?" Vicente asked again. "You've got something else

in your head. You might as well spit it out before your head explodes and I have to tell your parents."

"They're your parents too, *'Cente.*" She rolled her eyes, a customary gesture that all younger siblings knew and used to their advantage. "I have an idea of what we can do after you get whatever information you can from the suspect."

Silence settled amongst them for a moment before Vicente spoke. "You might as well say it, Pilar. We're listening."

Nodding, she looked at both of them and started to explain. "We can't play this defensive tactic forever. If we want to find out who is coming after Sloane, we're going to have to dive right in and stir up the waters."

Sloane wasn't exactly sure what Pilar was talking about, but the younger woman's enthusiasm went a long way to helping sway Sloane to her argument before she'd even made her whole suggestion.

"We're going to have to be more proactive and bring these people to us."

"Pilar..."

Sloane could feel Vicente tense up through their joined hands.

"We can't just wait for them to make a move, that would drag this out forever. What we need is to bring them to us so we end this once and for all."

Sloane saw the narrow-eyed look that Vicente gave his sister, as if she'd said something she shouldn't have, but she wasn't going to let the opportunity go.

"I don't see why we can't hear her plan later. I don't like having this target on my back. If we can find the men responsible this way, then let's do it. I know," she gave him a smile that she hoped looked easy and honest, "that you can't wait to get off of babysitting duty and get back to your job."

He gave her a slow nod as he watched her carefully.

Straightening her spine, Sloane knew she had to show him that she wasn't going to wilt when she was afraid.

"I have a few open cases that I need to finish ."

"See?" Sloane purposefully added a brighter tone to her voice. "Then it's decided. You go to the hospital to help them question the suspect and when you come back, we'll talk about Pilar's plan."

She stood up suddenly, almost falling over with the sudden change in position. Lord knows she hadn't planned to do it.

But she needed to get out of the room before she made a liar out of herself.

"If you'll both excuse me, I need to go to the restroom."

She didn't wait for anyone to say anything, she lifted her head and walked out of the room.

CHAPTER 11

When the on-call doctor made them leave the suspect's hospital room, Cruz and Vicente didn't go far, congregating on the other side of the hallway a few feet down. There were two uniformed officers on the door, but both agents kept throwing looks in that direction as they went over his answers.

Cruz leaned against the hallway wall. "You believe him?"

"Call me crazy, but yeah. I do." Vicente pushed his fingers through his hair, rumpling the front. "They left him to die, Cruz. He may be an ass and a criminal, but he's pissed. And he doesn't like the idea of spending the rest of life in prison when they didn't even pay him."

A sardonic smile answered him. "No honor among thieves, as they say, but there's a special kind of hell for men who sell people."

"And go after people trying to help others?" Vicente felt the bitter taste of bile on the back of his tongue. "I can't believe they're saying that Sloane brought this on herself. What has she done but give? Instead of using her family's fortune to live an easy life, she uses the money to help women and children in trouble."

"It's not fair, Vicente. None of this has anything to do about fairness."

"Then it should be about justice." He seethed with anger. "Criminals should suffer, but not her. Not like this. Good deeds should be rewarded."

Cruz nodded. "The people behind this are like hundreds of others that we've hunted down. And you have to believe that we're going to get these men and bring them to justice for what they've done. For what they're trying to do."

"How do you deal with all of this? I'm new to the task force, but you've been on it for a few months. How do you see the evil that these people are doing and not lose control?"

"Who says I do? Inside I rage and scream, but those moments are also the moments when I'm trying to comfort a child torn from its mother. Or a woman so bruised and battered she wants to die rather than go to a hospital for care.

"And women, torn from their families and sold to men who will pay thousands to own them, but don't care for them at all. I hate every minute, but I know that we're going to do good in this community. For the people we have a duty to protect."

A momentary image of Sloane stuffed into the back of a van, bound and gagged, stabbed him in the heart. It was an irrational fear, but it was there all the same. "I want to get back to Sloane."

Cruz looked up at him with a knowing grin. "Getting a little attached, are we?"

"No." Vicente felt like he'd been doused with cold water. "That's not why I want to get back. I don't think I can do much more here. If the doctor keeps us out for much longer,

I think we're just wasting time. We have enough to go on for now."

He waited for Cruz to say something, but the other man just folded his arms across his chest and focused his eyes on Vicente, narrowing them by degrees.

"Those eyes don't work on me."

Cruz's smile called bullshit. "You talked."

A muscle ticked in Vicente's cheek. "You're an ass."

"Hey," Cruz lifted a shoulder in a half-shrug, "I see what I see. And what I see is that you're in deep."

Lifting his chin by a degree, Vicente offered an answer. "I'm doing my job."

Cruz's smile was telling, like the cat that ate the canary. All that was missing was a stupid yellow feather peeking out at the corner. "You're falling for her."

Vicente's hands fisted at his sides and Cruz leaned back an inch.

"Don't kill the messenger. You're not that dense, *'Cente*." Cruz sighed. "You forget, I was undercover when I fell for Mickie. Falling for a woman someone wants you to kill can throw a bucketful of cold water on a fire, but I knew deep down that she was it for me."

Cruz passed an assessing glance over him and he was determined not to flinch.

"It's not the same. You and Mickie, you two fit together. Sloane is..." his gesture was vague at best, "she's so much more... deserves more than I can give her."

The look on his friend's face bothered him and Vicente turned away.

"Don't try to convince me otherwise. She's royalty in San Antonio, man. I'm just-"

"The man that's putting himself between her and a bullet?"

Vicente waved off his friend's words. "If we went by that,

she should be shacking up with that rookie cop that was shot at the accident site."

The words that came out of Cruz's mouth turned the head of a nurse walking down the hall. Her pale cheeks flushed with color and she looked away in shock.

"You're determined to be dense, so I'm not going to argue with you."

Vicente's shoulders sagged in relief.

"You're running on scared and stupid when it comes to Sloane. It'll work for now that she's got a target painted on her forehead, but when this is over and the adrenaline that's pounding through your veins is gone… then you'll have to figure it out for yourself." Cruz pushed away from the wall and took a step back. "Are you going to let her walk out of your life, or are you going to realize the truth?"

He didn't want to ask, but as he watched Cruz turn toward the hospital room, the question burst from his lips.

"What is the truth?" he asked his friend. "What do you see?"

Cruz tossed him a look over his shoulder. "You know. You're just afraid to admit it, and Vicente?"

"Yeah," he growled the answer at Cruz.

"Keep lying to yourself and someone's bound to get hurt. Don't put her through that. She doesn't deserve it. And neither do you."

Cruz stepped inside to speak to the doctor, leaving Vicente alone in the hallway.

And alone is exactly what he didn't need at the moment. Alone meant that his thoughts were much too loud in his head.

Slipping his phone out of his jeans pocket, he called his sister.

"Hey, what's up?"

He shook his head at her upbeat greeting, so much the

opposite of his own mood. "We were able to get some information. If you ever want a suspect to talk, remind him how his buddies left him for dead and he ends up talking more than you do."

Vicente knew the look on her face, he didn't have to see it in front of him. He'd seen it too many times to count growing up.

"I'm going to forget you said that because you're going to bring us *Las Quesadillas*. Apparently, you took Sloane there and now she's hooked, craving them like you wouldn't believe."

He laughed, but the sound scratched in his throat. He didn't need a reminder of what she looked like biting into a bit of cheese-filled heaven. He'd replayed the images in his mind a time or two... or ten, but he wasn't counting.

"Okay, so if I bring *Las Quesadillas* home, I won't get a kick to my shins?"

All he heard was a non-committal sound that said the jury was still out.

"How is she?"

There was a beat of silence. "*She*," Pilar cleared her throat, "is looking at me, probably wondering why you didn't call her after you talked to the suspect."

"*She*," he mimicked his sister's tone, "is probably wondering why you're talking about her like she's not in the room. Pick at me all you want, *Chiquita*, but don't be rude to Sloane."

"Hey," her tone held a note of resignation in it, "I know. Seriously, we're okay. Did you get enough information to-"

"I'll tell you both when I get there, okay?"

Pilar's end of the conversation was quiet for a moment. "Yeah, okay."

"Is something wrong? Pilar? Let me talk to him."

He winced when he heard the concern in Sloane's voice.

He was joking to keep his temper under control, but Sloane didn't know that. And if he heard his sister's tone correctly, she wasn't exactly blowing off the tension on her end.

"Let me talk to Sloane for a second."

He heard a few muffled sounds and then, "Vicente? What's going on? Did you talk to the man?"

"Hey," he forced himself to smile to lift his tone enough to ease her worry, "hey… calm down, everything's going to be okay. I'm going to grab us some food and I'll be home before you know it."

He heard a soft chuckle and knew that she was laughing at herself.

"Good. I'll feel better when I can see you."

Her words hit him square in the chest, but he told himself not to read into them. He had a job to do.

"Stay with Pilar. Feel free to irritate her as much as you like. She'll love every minute."

Now he heard the laugh he was hoping for. Soft, but full of humor and maybe a little joy.

"I'm so not going to do that. Your sister would kick my ass and love every minute."

"That's right," he heard Pilar's voice in the distance, "and I'm damn good at it. Bring the food!"

The call ended a moment later and Vicente dropped his phone back into his pocket. Shaking off the knowing look that Cruz sent him through the large glass window, he walked off down the hall.

❧

It took several days to get all the local Agencies to fall into step with each other. Vicente had given Sloane precious little information and that was really weighing on her mind.

Vicente had kept to his promise and she'd had plenty of time to visit and work at the center, but there seemed to be something 'odd' in his behavior.

Now, she didn't have any real knowledge of how law enforcement worked, who did what and when, but there was this thinly-veiled tension in the way he moved around her, around her apartment.

Sloane had asked him about it, but he told her it was nothing.

"Nothing for you to worry about."

To her, the words meant something. The way he said them meant something.

And there had been enough secrets in her life. With her parents they hid much of the dirtier aspects of business from their children, choosing to present a very rosy appearance whenever the girls visited their father at the office.

They didn't see the cold and calculated side of the business.

The edge that made their father a man most considered a 'shark' in San Antonio. The Kings had family money that they'd inherited, but her father had always told Sloane that just 'having' money wasn't enough. People with money had a responsibility to either make more money, instead of resting on their laurels, or to spend their money for a purpose.

He had endless stories ancestors in the King family tree. He especially loved how ancestors had funded good works and businesses in Texas as long as the family had lived on the soil of what had become the Lone Star State.

And it was those stories that Sloane had taken to heart, even if she preferred the stories of building schools and taking in widows and orphans to the stories of cattle barons fighting hand to hand against rustlers to recover their beeves.

But it wasn't until after her parents' deaths that she realized that much of what her father did in the name of business was but one step removed from what one might call 'cutthroat' deals.

Oh, he'd never done anything criminal as far as she could tell when she read between the lines, but her father, the great Robert King, had ridden that line as well as he'd ridden horses. And Robert had been a damn good rider.

The secrets only continued with her sister. Kimberly had learned from their father, or perhaps it was just part of the King family DNA that Sloane didn't inherit with as much veracity as her father and sister. Still, Kimberly was a master of secrecy.

No one played hide-and-go-seek like Kimberly Macy King.

And no one hid dangers and sometimes illegal activities like her sister.

Underage drinking? Check.

Pills and pot? Check.

Sex? Check, check, & check.

Still, there was one thing that Kimberly didn't hide from Sloane, that was how much she loved her.

The King sisters loved each other to Pluto and back.

Sloane shook her head to distract herself from the prickle of tears in her eyes. Her sister hadn't even lived long enough to know they'd demoted their favorite planet.

On one of the few nights when their parents had grounded their free-bird and kept her home, Kimberly had cuddled up with Sloane in her little double bed and they'd held each other close.

She doubted that Kimberly had known that her little sister was awake when she'd started to cry.

Gathering Sloane in her arms, Kimberly had pressed what seemed like a hundred kisses on Sloane's head and wrapped her arms securely around Sloane's much smaller form.

"Don't ever, ever, doubt that I love you, *Slo*. You're the sweetest thing in my pitiful life and if it's the last thing I ever do," she'd gasped in a breath and pulled Sloane so tight against her that it was a miracle that Sloane kept still enough to hear the rest of Kimberly's words, "I'm not going to let anyone hurt you. You hear that, baby sis? I'm going to protect you with every single breath."

A few months later, Sloane's life had changed.

Her parents had died in a random car crash and their Uncle Glen had moved the girls in with him. Sloane had hated every minute of it. All their things were back at the house and she wanted to feel like her parents were still there with them.

She couldn't feel them at Uncle Glen's house. And Kimberly, she had grown even more sullen and dark in her moods.

So, they'd hired a live in nanny of sorts and only Kimberly made visits to Uncle Glen's after that.

And then when Kimberly died...

"Hey."

She felt Vicente's warm hand on her leg and she lifted her head from her knees to look at him. Mustering a smile, she lifted her hand and smoothed his hair back from his forehead.

As hot as Vicente was when he was all badass FBI Special Agent, when he was lying in her bed, naked under her sheets, he called to the better, purer parts of her soul.

She couldn't help but think all of this would be over as soon as they found the men responsible and put them in jail.

"You've gone missing again."

Sloane blinked and shook herself slightly to clear her head of the fog. "Sorry, I was thinking."

He pushed an arm under his body and managed to lean over and plant a kiss on her shoulder. "I don't mind if you're thinking, but whatever it was in your head was making you sad."

She laughed, trying to fool both of them. "I worry. It's my thing."

He pushed himself up even more and sat beside her, the sheet pooling low on his hips. Vicente set his hand on her shoulder, lightly tapping the tips of his fingers along the thin silk strap of her tank, working it toward the edge of her shoulder. "What can I do to take your mind off of your worries?"

She closed her eyes and let the sensations wash over her, giving into the distraction just the littlest bit.

When she felt his breath fan over her shoulder she froze. When his teeth gently brushed against her as he tried to pluck the strap from her skin, her eyes flew open.

She hated to break the mood, especially when a quick look in his direction showed her just how into this he was, tenting the sheet over his lap, still… he'd been distracting her like this for days.

As her strap fell from his teeth, she picked it up with her fingers and set it back in place.

"Something wrong?"

She heard his guarded tone and prepared herself for the fight.

"What aren't you telling me?"

A moment passed before he smiled and leaned in against her arm. "You mean how good you look this morning? Or how much I loved making you scream last night?"

She couldn't help the rush of liquid heat that surged through her at the memory of the night before, tangled in his arms as he made her crazy with need.

But, she could tamp it down. She could remember that

there was something she needed at the moment more than an orgasmic trip down memory lane.

When he slipped his hand between her back and her tank, she turned toward him, tucking her legs beneath her, and focusing on the strong lines of his face.

"Why won't you level with me? Tell me what's going on?"

His expression lost any hint of a smile and he let out a long, heavy sigh. "Because I can't, baby."

Vicente let his hand fall to the mattress behind her, just the tips of two fingers grazing the curve of her backside.

"There are things I can't tell you. All you have to do is know that this is going to be over soon."

This.

Something pinched at the back of her neck, making her shiver a little.

"We have a plan in place to catch them in the act. The suspect we have in custody gave us enough information that we think we can beat them at their own game."

She nodded. "Okay. And what game is that?"

He blew a breath out of the corner of his mouth, lifting the very ends of his hair that had fallen beside his temple. "You're not going to give up on this, are you?"

Leaning forward, she cupped her hands against his jaw and felt the subtle scratch of his hair against her palms. "If I was keeping a dangerous secret from you," she rose up on her knees just enough to touch her lips to his mouth, "would you want to know what it was?"

He shifted positions on the bed, getting up on his hands and knees to return her kiss, pressing into her until she sat back down.

Once she was there, he pulled back slightly, enough to look into her eyes.

"If it involved you being in danger? Absolutely."

"Well-"

"But I'm not in any danger, baby. They train us well, you know."

Her expression told him exactly what she thought about his words, and it wasn't pretty.

"I'm just worried because I can feel how much this is bothering you, Vicente."

He moved closer, spreading his legs just enough to cage her between them.

"The only thing bothering me is the idea that there are still people out there trying to hurt you and stop the good that you're doing."

She tried to brush off his concern. "I don't need the money that my family made and saved all of these years. I have enough to live off of and some to take care of me when I'm older, the rest," she sighed, "can do more good for others than it can do for me. The last thing I want to do is give up the foundation, but if the people we serve might be hurt because of all of this… then I would. But right now, my concern is you. What kind of danger you're going to be in."

He reached out and set his hands on her hips and pulled her up onto his lap.

Sloane wrapped her legs around him and lightly crossed her ankles, pressing her as close as she could get to him.

Vicente groaned and slid his hands around to her backside, smoothing his hands over her curves as he spoke. "I can't give you all the details, but what I can tell you is that we think we have enough information to do a sting. We're going to put several undercover officers and agents in the area that the men are likely to target for new victims. We'll have separate teams covering the undercover women, and we're confident that we'll pull these men out of hiding and they will then lead us to the man who's running the show. Once we get him into custody, his whole organization is likely to disintegrate. We think we'll pick up many of them before they can go into hiding and when all is said and done, you'll be safe. You can continue on with what you do so well, and your life can go back to normal."

She nodded, slowly, and her eyes closed as she considered her next words. "And your life?" Knowing it was too vague, she added a few words. "What will your life be like when it goes back to normal?" She felt her teeth grind together. Her words were still too vague, but they were all she had. Then again, she was used to being inadequate at times like these.

"Me?" He cupped her closer, rocking slightly against the apex of her thighs. "My 'normal' is a job with somewhat regular hours that is sometimes frustrating and still satisfying. I have a family that likes to stick their nose into my business much too much for my own peace of mind. They're pushing me to follow the example set up by my eldest brother and sister. Find the perfect woman. Marry her and have a ton of babies with her so my nieces and nephews can have even more playmates. Although, at this point, my mother might just overlook if the babies are started before the wedding."

Sloane swallowed against the lump in her throat. She hadn't thought of children in years. She'd made such a mess of her life, children didn't seem to be a good idea, or even in the cards.

"And you want a bunch of kids?" She heard the squeak in her voice and looked away when his eyes tried to search hers. "Not that it's any of my business, but-"

He silenced her with a kiss, rubbing the tip of his tongue against her lower lip before he leaned back again.

"You're so adorable when I shock you into silence." He smiled at her. "It has everything to do with you, Sloane. I know I've been distracted lately, and you've had to deal with a number of other agents and police as security, but it wasn't because I don't want to be here.

"I want to be here. I want to be around you as much as I can, and I hope that after this is all over and the level of adrenaline in your veins goes back to its every day levels crazy busy levels, you won't look at me and ask yourself 'what the hell was I thinking letting him anywhere near me?'"

She lifted her hands and looped them around the back of his neck. "Vicente, I-"

"Just let me explain," he urged her. "What's been happening between us… I've never felt anything like this before. I've never been with a woman who holds me the way you do. And I'm not talking about the way you hold me close when we're making love, baby. I'm talking about the way you look at me. The way you touch me and try to take care of me.

"I'm not going to want this to end. In fact," he drew his hands around to her waist and brushed his thumbs against the sides of her belly, "I want to see where all of this goes. I want to romance you until the only person you'll ever want in your bed and in your heart is me."

She looked down as he shifted a hand, flattening his palm against her body and around to the area of skin just beneath her bellybutton.

"And if you don't come to your senses and go out and marry a doctor, or a lawyer, or any other man who would probably be better for you, I want to have babies with you."

Her breaths were shallowing out, her heart pounding so loud in her chest and she heard it in her ears.

"You want babies with me." She repeated the words again, but it still didn't seem real. "Why?"

"Because, I love you, Sloane King." His smile disarmed her and the way he looked down at his hand on her body and licked at his lips made her wet and achy between her thighs. "You probably think I'm crazy for saying it. Or that I'm not serious. But you need to know that I don't throw those words around. I've never said them to anyone not already related to me by blood.

"I love your face, your heart, and you know I love your body, but we're not going to talk about anything more until this is over and you're not going to think I'm just saying this for any other reason than because I mean it."

"I-"

He pulled her in for another kiss, slanting his mouth over hers, and she let him, because she knew when it was all over, he'd realize that the woman he'd fallen for wasn't who she really was.

The brave soul he thought he held in his arms was nothing more than a woman desperate to keep herself together.

A woman so afraid of being alone that she gave of herself until she wasn't sure there was anything left.

And if Vicente Bravo believed for a minute that he loved her, she was going to let him.

It was a heady feeling to have his lips on hers and his hands sliding up under her tank, lifting the supple fabric until he cradled her aching breasts. She would let him make love to her and when this was all over, she'd at least have these memories to hold onto.

And maybe she wouldn't feel so lonely any more.

But would that be enough?

CHAPTER 12

When the guard changed at Sloane's apartment, everything went just as it always did. The uniformed guard coming off duty went inside to sign out and then left a few minutes later.

And about an inch shorter.

It was the late afternoon sun that made it hard to see the exact features of the officer as she left the building and climbed into a patrol car waiting just outside of the lobby door. Sliding into the passenger seat, the officer bumped her hat on the door frame and had to make a grab for it before it fell off her head.

The curse that spat from her lips earned her a laugh from her driver.

"Well, make you an officer for an hour and you're already swearing like the best of us."

Sloane turned to look at Deputy Hayden Hatcher and sighed out loud. "I'm sorry if you got the incorrect opinion of me earlier."

The Deputy gave her a quick sideways glance as she pulled away from the curb at a moderate speed. "What do you mean?"

Leaning on her armrest, Sloane smiled at the deputy, enjoying the presence of the no-nonsense deputy. "When I met you the other day with Vicente and Pilar, I don't think you got a look at the real me."

Turning on a blinker, the driver, Deputy Hayden Hatcher, eased into a turn lane, taking a look into the rearview mirror. "Our backup team is behind us, no sign of a tail." When they were safely onto the next street, she looked over at Sloane. "What do you mean the 'real' you? Are you some kind of alien creature from Mars?"

The corners of her mouth quirked up in reply. "Nope, men are from Mars-"

"So you're from Venus!"

The two women laughed and Sloane sighed again, feeling more tension ease from her body. "I'm from somewhere on the crazy train. But really, I'm not any different than anyone else. I get blisters from my shoes, I have horrible nails, and when it comes to swearing, let me stub my toe and you'll hear a pretty thorough vocabulary of curse words. My sister was a great teacher."

Hayden gave her an understanding smile. "I get it. It's just that growing up in San Antonio, we saw your picture in the news and in the paper just as much as we saw the English Royals. It was like we watched you grow up."

Sloane turned back to look through the windshield. "You mean you watched me grow up and everything implode around me." She shifted on the seat. "Don't get me wrong, it's all water under the bridge now, but I'm sure you saw moments in my life when I was at my worst."

After they crossed through an intersection, Hayden drove the car into the parking lot behind the police station.

"Don't get me wrong, Sloane. We saw what you were going through. It must have been like walking through hell for you. While some people must have enjoyed seeing someone in the public eye go through something like that, some people are jerks.

"I should know, I arrest enough of them."

She brought the car to a stop beside a champagne colored Lexus which Sloane recognized as Hildie's car.

"Still, I want you to know that there were those of us who saw you and heard about your family and grieved along with you. You didn't deserve to suffer like that. I just hope that when this is done, you can start a new part of your life. A happier one."

Sloane blinked way the tears that had gathered on her lashes. "Thank, Hayden." Sloane reached across the car and gave the deputy's arm a gentle squeeze. "That means a lot."

Hayden waved off her thanks. "Don't make me get all mushy. Go on, get inside. Your friend is waiting in one of the conference rooms. I think she brought in half of a nail salon. My commanding officer has been holed up in his office since she arrived."

"Sounds like Hildie." Sloane opened her door and stepped out. "Thanks again, Hayden. Be safe out there."

The deputy nodded and agreed. "My husband tells me the same thing before I leave for work every day."

"That's good," Sloane conceded, "you're a lucky woman."

Sloane was about to close the door when Hayden leaned over. "Don't I know it. I'll see you later."

❧

Vicente looked up as the front door opened and a handful of people stepped inside the bar. There was a big 'Closed for Private Function' sign on the outside of the bar and the lights in the front of the bar were set as low as they could go to keep curious eyes from the outside from seeing that there were maybe a handful of people posing as partygoers.

The newest additions were female officers dressed up for a night on the town, but in outfits that weren't too expensive or showy. They were going to be bait and bait had to look available and alone.

All the women were volunteers and were either experienced with vice or narcotics and were used to working on the street, knew their procedures like the back of their hands.

He was about to look back down at his notes when one last woman slipped in through the door.

"Pilar?"

She caught his eye and smiled. "Hey there! I was going to come find you, but it looks like I don't have to work too hard. I'm just that good."

He walked around the fold out table and gave his sister a hug. "What are you doing here?"

She leaned back in his embrace. "Cassie was supposed to come down and help and she ended up with a stomach bug. I didn't want you to be short one, so I came down."

He couldn't help the slight wince in his expression. "Sloane's not going to like this."

Pilar slugged him on his shoulder, making him wince even more. "By the time your girlfriend finds out that I worked the sting, it will be over and done with and she'll be mad, but she won't worry. So suck it up, *hermano*."

When he didn't immediately shoot back with his own comment, Pilar gave him a strange look and he knew she had him under her microscope. The main problem was that she was just too damn good at it.

"Besides," she quipped, "it's all your fault anyway. You could have assigned me to watch her tonight, but you didn't. So, I was completely free to join in with the other scantily clad and seemingly economically downtrodden women walking the streets tonight." She seemed to ignore his pointed glare. "So, tell me. Where is Sloane tonight? Locked in a bank vault somewhere?"

"Kind of. Something like. She's sitting in a conference room at the station across town with her friend Hildie for company."

"That sounds mind-numbingly boring." She shook her head at her brother. "Stuck in a station house? Couldn't you have gotten her some overnight spa treatment or something?"

Vicente struggled to remind himself that he couldn't kill his sister. Pity. "Unless you could refer me to a spa that has armed guards, no. I didn't send Sloane to a spa."

His sister gave him a curious look and then let out a soft chuckle. "I hope tonight goes off without a hitch, because if it doesn't you're going to explode."

"Explode?"

"You are wound so tight, *'Cente*. Once this is over, you should consider taking Sloane away for a weekend so you two can... explode together."

He saw the look on Pilar's face. The mischievous light in her eyes.

"Remind me again of why I love you?"

She wrapped her arms around his neck and whispered into his ear. "Because I'm just that fabulous. Now, I'm going to go and get dressed... or rather 'undressed' and you are likely going to go over the plans another ninety-eight times before we gather up to go over the operation in about," she looked up at the wall, "twenty minutes. So go," she gestured to the makeshift desk, "get back to work and I'm heading for the bathroom."

❧

It had taken about twenty minutes for Sloane to regret that she asked Hildie to sit with her while Vicente was working on the sting in the old warehouse district. After being around Vicente day in and day out, Hildie's frenetic energy had quickly worn her down.

She had almost considered it a welcome change from Hildie's ramble when she asked Sloane about Vicente.

It started out easy and innocent enough. Talking about the simple everyday things that they'd done together, and before she knew it, she was delving into feelings she had been desperately trying to hide.

And feelings she was too afraid to believe. "He said that when this," she gestured at their surroundings, "is over, he wants to continue to see me. So we can see where this can go."

"See you?" Hildie set her elbows down on the table and touched her chin to her folded hands. "If I'm reading you right, sweetie, he's done more than 'see' you."

Sloane felt her cheeks warm and didn't even try to deny it. Hildie knew her too well. "We've been… close."

"You've done the deed!" Hildie clapped her hands together. "Hallelujah!"

Sloane gave her a look that promised death, or at least a little dismemberment between friends. "Shush."

"Was it good?" She waved off the thought. "Of course it was good! Was it… awesome? Toe curling? Did he talk dirty? Did *you* talk dirty? Please tell me he bent you over the nearest piece of furniture and made you scream in six different languages."

Her final question faded into silence, but Sloane didn't say a word. She just sat there, wide-eyed and still.

"Oh wow. I think I broke her." She leaned forward and

waved her hand in front of Sloane's face. "Sweetie? Can you hear me?"

Smacking her palm on the table, Sloane leaned in to speak to her friend. "I'm fairly sure everyone in the building can hear you. Will you shush?"

Touching a hand to her chest, Hildie reared back in shock that almost looked real enough to believe. "I am offended at your tone, Miss King."

Sloane leaned back heavily in her chair. "First, I'm sorry, but there's no way I'm going to believe that you are offended, so you can drop the act. Second, if this was any other night together at your place or mine and if we had a bottle of wine on the table and nightshirts with outrageous words on them, sure. I'd probably be telling you a few amazing details just to hear you squeel.

"But tonight, my stomach is tied up in knots and I just have this feeling."

"Forget that feeling in your stomach and talk to me about the organ just a little higher than that."

"Organ?" Sloane shuddered.

"What?" Hildie rolled her eyes. "I remember some of anatomy class that didn't have to do with sex. So, he wants this to be real… to continue after tonight. You haven't told me how you feel. What do you want from him?"

Sloane didn't want to talk about it much longer, but Hildie was her oldest and dearest friend, and that deserved at least a couple of answers. "I'm not sure I know what it's like to love a man the way he wants me to love him. I'm not sure I have it in me after what happened to Kimberly. Losing her so soon after losing our parents made everything hurt. Like someone came and cut me up from head to toe in a thousand little slashes and then dropped me in saltwater.

"I hurt inside and out. I cried on and on for days and then

weeks, until I don't remember how long I'd gone on. I don't think I have the capacity to open myself up to that again."

"Why are you worried, Sloane? He hasn't demanded a declaration of love, has he?"

She shook her head first, summoning up the words to explain. "No. He hasn't, but-"

"But nothing! If you ask me, and I'm going to pretend that you did, you're just borrowing trouble. He said he wants to see where this… I mean where the two of you… are going. That's a pretty simple, and yet meaningful thing from him. Hell, from any man."

Sloane had to agree with her. She just kept it quiet. Giving Hildie too much rope meant that she'd be dragging Sloane with it every chance she got.

Hildie continued. "Are you going to tell me what you said in return?"

"If I'd been thinking straight, I probably would have told him that I needed time to think."

"But he was probably distracting you with all of that hot FBI mojo like Mulder from X-files."

"Something like that."

Hildie gestured in the air, circling her hand around and around. "And…"

"And, I told him I was going to take that chance if that's what he wants too."

Hildie reached out and grabbed Sloane's hand so hard that Sloane winced.

"Hildie, sweetie? You're going to break my hand."

Instead of releasing it right away, Hildie only pulled her close and pressed a kiss on the back of her hand. "That's my girl."

Sloane managed to extricate her hand from Hildie's. "There's nothing set in stone," she reminded her friend. "We said we'd try to see if this is going to go somewhere."

"I'm sorry," Hildie tilted her head to the side and stared at her friend, "what is this try thing?"

Sloane shrugged. "We're not sure where this is going. Things have happened... really fast."

Her friend grinned ear to ear. "Nothing wrong with that, considering that you haven't had any for years-"

"You promised never to bring that up."

"And who is here to hear it besides the two of us?"

She wanted to tell Hildie more about her feelings for Vicente. She wanted to tell her best friend that he'd told her he loved her, but she wasn't ready for a conversation about that now. Not with this whole operation coming to a head. "Really, I don't want to talk about Vicente right now, I feel like I'm trying to stand up on that balance beam from PE, and you know I'm just going to land on my butt the instant I look away."

"*Oookay,*" Hildie spoke slowly and lowered her voice to nearly a whisper, "then what are we going to talk about?"

"Anything that's not about my life."

"Way to narrow the scope of conversation, girlfriend."

"I just don't want to jinx things."

Hildie snatched up one of the magazines she had dumped onto the table and paged through, desperately looking for something to focus on. "Oh!" She turned the magazine around and gave Sloane a big teeth-baring grin. "Jason Momoa." Hildie waited for Sloane's reaction and finally sat back with a little huff. "Honey, if you can't even get excited over Jason, you've got it bad for your agent."

Sloane rolled her eyes. "Keep pushing those buttons, Hildie."

"Oh," she pinked in her cheeks, "that's bringing it back to your life. Sorry."

Sloane walked along the windowed wall of the conference room and watched the police outside as they went about their evening. The late shift meant there weren't a lot of people outside, but it might be just enough to keep her mind off that feeling in the pit of her stomach.

Outside of their glass windowed enclosure, Sloane saw two deputies jump up from their desks and rush outside. She tried to focus on the sounds she could hear from the main room. There wasn't much to go on, but she did see people looking up at the speakers.

The knot was suddenly a stone in her gut, weighing heavily on her.

She pulled her phone out of her back pocket and stared at the screen.

Vicente wasn't running the sting, neither was Cruz. The Director of the local FBI Field Office, Jack Travis, was in charge to allow the others to focus on their specific functions within the command center.

From what she understood, the operation wouldn't start for at least another hour. Looking through her contacts she decided to call Cruz.

If she called Vicente he'd only worry about her and she wanted, no, she needed him to focus.

Sloane called Hildie's name softly and her friend looked up with a smile. "I'm going to step out and go to the restroom. I'll be right back."

Hildie rolled her eyes. "I can get you a police escort."

Groaning at the comment, Sloane moved into the hallway and when she was sure she was out of sight from all the windows in the conference room she looked up a name in her contacts and touched the icon

The call was answered after a handful of rings. "Sloane? Is everything okay?"

"Fine, Cruz. I just wanted to call and see how things are going. I didn't want to worry Vicente, but it sounds like I made you worry too."

His laughter was warm and gentle. "Well, the longer you're with Vicente, you'll begin to understand. We have a network of friends in the San Antonio area and more, extending all the way across the country with not only First Responders but military units as well. We're all what you might call… fiercely protective of our loved ones."

"So, you're all stubborn as hell."

He laughed again. "Absolutely. And we don't joke or play games with safety. Nothing would stop us from doing everything we could to protect our women."

"And you know that your women likely do just as much to protect you right back, don't you?"

Another laugh. "Has anyone ever told you that you're too smart for your own good?"

A cold chill passed through her. "I've heard that a few times in my life."

"You want me to deliver a message to your man?"

Your man.

The sound of it felt good and she reveled in it for a moment until the odd sensation coursed through her veins again.

"No. I just needed to hear that things were going well."

"They are." She heard the reassuring tone in his voice and latched onto it like a lifeline. "I think it was a surprise when Pilar walked in a little earlier."

"Pilar?" Sloane felt nauseous when wave after wave of fear rolled over her like waves against rocks. "She's not supposed to be there."

"Well, things change on stings like this. One of the volunteer vice officers was unable to make it in and Pilar took her place. Don't worry about Vicente's sister. She's tough as nails and she's been trained well. Beyond that, she knows when to fight dirty."

"Can't someone else step in for her?" Sloane's head ached.

"Sloane?" She heard the sharp edge of his concern. "What's wrong?"

"Pilar is his sister. Shouldn't he want her out of danger?"

"I think he felt that way when she was fresh out of the academy. Make no mistake, Sloane, Pilar knows what she's doing. We all do."

"Oh, I know." She felt horrible for making him think she didn't. She just couldn't manage to find the words to tell him what she felt.

It seemed so odd to have these feelings again.

The same unsettled stomach and pounding head the night that Kimberly died. What if she didn't say something... try something... and Pilar was hurt or worse?

Could she live with herself then?

Would it kill the chance that they had at a future?

Sloane pushed away the selfish worries and mumbled a reply to Cruz before she hung up the phone.

She had no idea what she was going to do, but she knew she had to do something. For her to stay there and wait was no longer a possibility.

Leaning back against the wall, Sloane started to formulate a plan.

CHAPTER 13

After Director Travis introduced Cruz and Vicente to the assembled group, he left it to his agents to go over the finalized plans for the sting operation.

Cruz finalized the groups, dividing up local deputies and FBI officers, detailing EMT placement and distress codes. Once those details were covered, he turned to Vicente.

"I'm sure all of you saw the coverage of the accident that started this whole operation," he saw the group nod and exchange knowing looks, "we have one of the men in custody and the information he has given us is what's led us to tonight's sting.

"They'll be out trolling for women, looking for anyone alone… vulnerable. That's where we come in. We're going to be watching out for them. When they try to make their move, that's when we'll make ours. The important thing here is we all make it home to our families, our loved ones." He tried to swallow down the lump in his throat but couldn't get it down. "While you're out there be sharp, be safe, and let's get these guys off the streets."

The room erupted into movement. Groups formed up.

Introductions were made, and the room began to clear. Vicente stayed back as the Director went with Cruz to go over the map again. Taking the moment to himself, Vicente pulled his phone out from his back pocket and stared at the screen. He'd taken a picture of Sloane sitting with his sister at the dining table. They were laughing over someone's joke. The look of joy on both of their faces made this waiting easier.

He was going to figure this out. He was going to put these men away and make San Antonio safer for everyone.

And then Sloane could go back to her life, helping others and he could do the same. When they did spend time together, it wouldn't be because someone was trying to kill her. It would be because they wanted to be together.

That was the gift that Sloane had given him. A chance to look forward to time together.

Cruz sat down on the desk beside him. "You thinking of calling Sloane?"

Shaken from his thoughts, he shook his head and slid his phone back into his coat pocket. "I told Sloane that I'd call her when it was all over."

"That sounds like a plan." Cruz gave him a smile. "Once this is over, Mickie wants to have you both over for dinner."

"Sounds like a plan," Vicente admitted. "It'll be nice to take Sloane somewhere that isn't just going from one room to another or to her work. I'm looking forward to the opportunity to take her dancing or maybe even away for a weekend."

Cruz's smile only widened. "I like this look on you."

Vicente narrowed his gaze at his friend. "What look?"

"Happy."

Sloane did her best to keep her promise. She put her butt in a seat and tried to make small talk with Hildie. Tried to eat some of the snacks she'd brought and find a way to talk herself out of believing in her 'premonition.' After all, it wasn't even really a premonition, just a feeling that something was going to go wrong.

That didn't mean that something was… right?

Would've. Should've. Could've.

Sloane had lived so many years with those words in her head.

What if she would have called for some help to look for Kimberly when she'd first felt 'that' feeling?

She should have. She knew that for certain.

If she had, and the police had gone looking for her earlier, they could have found her. Earlier.

And if she read the coroner's report correctly, a few hours would have made all the difference.

Would have made all the difference.

From that moment, it took a heartbreaking minute for Sloane to realize that she was going to break her promise to Vicente, but she couldn't see that she had any other option.

The feeling of dread that had taken root in her belly wasn't going anywhere and there was no way that she was going to let something happen to his family just because her luck was always bad.

The cloud that had followed her for years had no right to latch itself onto Vicente. She wasn't going to let it.

If he was angry with her later, she'd deal with it, but she couldn't shake the feeling that if she didn't do anything, something horrible was going to happen to Pilar.

Unlocking her phone, she double checked to make sure she had Pilar's phone number in her contacts and then opened up the *FriendTrack* app. Turning it on she recognized the map immediately. Mr. Ordonez was more than happy to close his bar for a few days in exchange for having his rental fee cut in half for the month. The FBI had staged their command center in his bar.

Sloane wanted them to be as close to their Undercover operatives as possible to give them every opportunity to make the sting successful. As she watched, Pilar's icon moved out of the back door of the bar and continued down the back alley making her way to the next big cross street.

The alleyways in that part of town were narrow, barely wide enough for a smart car to drive down and back again. The buildings hadn't changed much since the early 1900s when building were made of brick and were closer together than they were in a more modern era.

While she wasn't sure where Pilar had been assigned to work that night, this app would give her a chance to find her friend.

She just had to get down there.

A deputy passed her in the hallway and gave her a curious look. "Do you need any help, Miss King?"

"No," she shook her head, "I just needed a moment to myself."

The man nodded and continued down the hallway.

Sloane knew she couldn't ask the deputies for a ride, they knew why she was there. Surely one of them would call Vicente if she tried to leave.

Tucking her phone away she went back to the conference room. When she opened the door a solid cloud of acetone assaulted her. Sloane leaned back and away from the smell. "What are you doing?"

Hildie looked up with the cotton swab still pinched between her fingers. "I brought everything we needed for a mani-pedi. When you were outside for forever I thought I'd start." She waved the cotton swab over her foot. "I know I'm usually such a spaz when it comes to doing my own nails, but I was feeling particularly awesome tonight and gave it a try."

"What happened?" Sloane moved closer and craned her neck to see. There was a large explosion of purple polish that started on one toe and then moved halfway onto the other. "Did you spill it from the bottle?"

Hildie rolled her eyes. "Did I spill it? Of course not. I was using the brush and then my iPod started that new Country song, you know the one that I can't stand and so I reached over to change it and when I leaned back, I'd apparently painted my toes."

"Like Tom Sawyer painting the fence?"

Hildie's eyes narrowed. "Is that some home improvement show?"

"Never mind."

Hildie had already moved on. "I put a ton of acetone on it, but it's still there. All over my skin. I don't know what I did wrong."

Neither did Sloane, but it was best to leave the worry to Hildie.

"Oh, I think I have something in the car that's stronger." Using her elbow, Hildie nudged the keys in her direction. "Here, do you think you could get me my tackle box out of the trunk."

"Tackle box?"

Hildie shook her head. "You know... my makeup kit."

"Oh, that. Sure."

Picking up the keys, Sloane was a step away from the door before she realized that Hildie had solved her problem. Looking from the office outside to Hildie's new make-up bunker, Sloane felt one piece of her plan fall into place.

Then again, it wasn't so much of a plan as it was a crazy random happenstance, but she was going to take hold of it and run. Moving back into the room she crossed to the far side and reached up for the pulley ropes along the side of one window. She had it completely down by the time Hildie noticed.

"What are you doing?"

"Well, the station is supposed to be for law enforcement. If we're going to sit in here and do our nails someone from the street might walk in and think we're fooling around on the public dime."

"I see," Hildie agreed. "Go ahead and shut the rest of the windows. I've got some movies on the phone we can watch when you get back from my car."

"Good plan." Sloane finished with the windows and came back around the table. She touched a gentle kiss on Hildie's cheek. "You're a really good friend, Hildie."

"I'm not, really," her protest was a little weak.

"Oh really? I thought you'd agree with me."

"I'm not a really good friend. I'm the best."

Sloane turned away and walked out the door with a smile on her face. This was going to work.

She would make it work.

❧

When the bar's phone rang, Cruz picked it up and listened. "Uh huh. Okay, hold on." He pressed the button on the phone. "I've got you on speaker, Hayden."

"Hey, how is everyone else doing?"

Vicente sat on the edge of the table and stretched his neck to one side. "It's like a ghost town out there. What about you?"

There was a non-committal huff of noise. "Bored. We haven't seen a suspicious vehicle or a shady guy anywhere. A couple here and there. Three obnoxious college aged girls who have some kind of Greek Letters on their sweaters."

"Sweaters?" Cruz cringed beside him. "In this weather?"

"Well," Deputy Haskell piped in, "they were drunk… so-"

"Anyway, Vicente, your sister is probably fifteen minutes away from either starting a fight with the next dude that palms her backside or taking out her phone and playing solitaire."

Vicente shook his head. "I don't understand why we haven't gotten even a bite." He and Cruz shared a look. "We grilled him."

Cruz nodded in agreement. "He couldn't have been that good of an actor. Besides, this is a Friday night. There should be more people."

"More action."

"I'm beginning to get a bad-"

"Don't say it." Vicente stuck a finger into his friend's chest. "Bite your tongue."

Hayden came back on the line. "As much as I love wearing this Kevlar vest," she chuckled, "are we sticking to the schedule? Taking this to the bitter end?"

Vicente saw Cruz's hesitant look. Together they turned to the Director.

"Sir?"

Jack Travis reached a hand up and scrubbed the back of his neck. "We've got everyone mobilized and put in place. Let's keep this going until the end. Every time we do an operation like this, we know there's a chance that the fish won't bite."

"Well," Hayden huffed, "then let's keep fishing and hope the bad guys get hungry."

Vicente nodded at Cruz and then his Director. "Okay, we keep going."

He ended the phone call and considered calling Sloane.

He didn't want to bother or worry her, but damn it if he didn't feel like he needed to hear her voice.

❧

Sloane knew she couldn't go back inside if she wanted this to work. So, she hoped that Hildie hadn't cleared out her trunk to bring all her nail supplies to the station.

Using the keychain fob she unlocked the little black Mini Cooper and lifted the trunk. One look at the boxes in the back of the trunk and Sloane let out a sigh of relief. Setting the keys down on top of one of the boxes, Sloane opened the crate that held clothing in it. Taking out a sweater, she pulled it over her clothes. The sweater was dark, and her pants were loose enough and dark enough to work in that neighborhood. There weren't enough lights on the streets to make it safe, but that would suit her purposes tonight.

The accessories crate had a bunch of different hats in it. Picking up the San Antonio Spurs cap and twisting up her hair onto the top of her head, she pulled the cap down to secure it in place.

Looking into the reflection in the back window of the car she gave herself a good hard look and nodded. This could work.

She was a heartbeat away from dropping the trunk down when she stopped. The small cardboard box nearest to the front of the trunk caught her eye.

Pulling the cover open she looked at the pair of phones laying in the chargers. Reaching into the box she pulled the first one out and pushed the power button. The phone flickered to life and the readout said that the power was 100%.

"All right," Sloane whispered to herself, "this is good. I can use this."

Lifting the hem of her hastily donned sweater she lifted her blouse up too and managed to tuck the tiny phone into the bottom of her bra cup, under the swell of her breast.

"Better safe than sorry," she muttered to herself, "even if it's uncomfortable as hell."

Shutting the trunk, she ducked around to the driver's side and opened the door. She set her phone down on the center console and shut the door, quickly buckling her seatbelt in before inserting the key.

"Okay. Let's do this."

❧

Cruz leaned back in his chair and shook his head. "Tell me I'm not the only one that thought this was going to be a slam dunk."

Vicente shook his head. "Maybe we waited too long. Maybe they realized he didn't die." He reached out for the phone and picked it up, dialing up the agent in charge of the safe house locations.

"Bravo? What's up?"

He was glad they didn't need to muddle through with pleasantries. "Our witness. Any news? Chatter?"

There was a momentary pause on the other end of the phone. "Hmm… not that we've heard. His mother's proceeding with funeral arrangements. She didn't challenge the mortuary employee who told her that it had to remain a closed-casket event."

"That was one of our guys, right?"

"Exactly. Henderson is getting so good at these appointments, the funeral home director asked him if he wanted a side job."

"Well, as long as they keep up appearances-"

"When he told me about the job offer I had to think about changing professions."

"Is that all?"

"The news? Yeah. Sure. No one seems to have any idea that your witness survived the bullet. Need anything else?"

Vicente met Cruz's eyes and shook his head. "No, I think we're good. Call me if anything changes."

"Absolutely, Bravo. You know I'm here for you. These bastards are just that and need to be stopped."

"Thanks." The call ended moments later and he shared the news with Cruz. "Everything looks good. No word from our informants about our witness."

Cruz shook his head. "And our informants have been good in the past, so here's hoping."

"Yeah, because that's about all we have left."

❧

Sloane found a parking spot along one side of the rundown park, two blocks away from Pilar's location. The playground structure was half-wrapped up in CAUTION tape and had been that way for a few months, but Sloane pulled her thoughts away from that problem to examine the one right in front of her.

Or rather, two blocks ahead and one to the right.

Silencing her phone, she dropped it into her pants pocket and stripped everything from Hildie's keychain except for the car key and the alarm fob. After all, the least she could do for her friend was hope that setting the alarm would deter anyone from stealing the car.

Leaving everything else behind, Sloane shut the door and set the alarm. Crossing over into the shadows, she started to walk with strides a little longer and a little faster from her normal pace.

She didn't want to draw attention to herself.

Sure, she had put on the largest sweater in the box, but she wasn't sure that would disguise her completely. She still had hips that a man wouldn't, but it was dark.

But she wasn't going to run and draw too much attention to herself. As her sister used to tell her on a regular basis, "You run like a girl."

She forced Kimberly out of her mind. There wasn't enough room in her head for old memories if she was going to concentrate on the present.

Turning the corner, she put her hand out and braced it against the wall. She sucked in a few breaths to fill her lungs. She hadn't been running but she'd move fast enough to put a little ache in her lungs and the muscles in her thighs.

Up ahead, a figure moved through the light from a wall fixture and Sloane focused her eyes on their form. Short in stature, curvy hips with a sassy sway.

Pilar.

"Oh, thank God."

One last replenishing breath and Sloane was on her way again. She crossed over a small side street, staying just out of the light from the streetlights in the intersection.

She turned her head as a car on the other side of the street started to move forward.

Keeping her hands at her side, but a good distance from her sides, she continued to move. The car was likely one of the backup cars with law enforcement officers inside. She didn't want them to think she was a threat to Pilar.

That would only complicate things.

A quick flash of color drew her eyes and she recognized the color for what it was. Deputy Hayden Hatcher was in the car. Lifting her chin a little, Sloane gave a low wave at the car and saw Hayden's stunned expression.

"Here goes nothing," she mumbled to herself. As soon as she stepped onto the curb she called out softly. "Pilar!"

The woman ahead stopped instantly and turned around, peering into the dark. "Sloane? What the hell are you doing?"

Sloane caught up to her friend and stopped short, trying to catch her breath again. Having her heart tied up in knots with her worried stomach didn't help matters. "I had to come and find you. You're not supposed to be working this operation."

"I know. I had to fill in for another officer. It's just fine." Pilar's smile was supposed to reassure her, but all Sloane could think about was how wrong all of this was.

"No," Sloane felt everything inside of her tense and twist with worry, "it's not, we have to get you out of here. Let's flag down Hayden and get you back to Vicente."

Pilar gently took hold of Sloane's arms and leaned closer. "Well we have to now. '*Cente* is going to flip when he finds out you're here. He's going to want to-"

The world shook and the ground beneath their feet rolled like a wave, lapping at them as if they were standing in the tide. It was only at that moment that Sloane realized that her ears were ringing. "What... what happened?"

CHAPTER 14

Sloane tried to shake her head to clear it of the overwhelming echo that banged around inside of her head.

Someone touched her face, cradling both cheeks.

She looked up and saw Pilar staring at her.

Blinking at her, Sloane heard vague sounds as Pilar moved her lips so she had to narrow her eyes to read her lips.

EXPLOSION

Sloane nodded and together they turned to look for Hayden's car. They saw them making the turn in the street to head their way. Sloane took Pilar's arm and together they started toward Hayden's car hoping to close the distance.

All Sloane wanted to do was get Pilar to her brother. From there, she'd deal with the rest.

She had a vague impression of Hayden's expression, stone serious… her jaw set in a hard line, her hands crawling over each other to turn the wheel in as tight a turn as she could. The person in the passenger seat was a stranger to her, but she saw him speaking into something, a phone or a radio. The car was almost facing in the right direction to pull up on their side of the street when bright lights flashed in her eyes.

Sloane held onto Pilar with one hand and managed to throw her other hand over her eyes, but the lights were so bright and intense, she couldn't see beyond the splotchy shadows that swam before her. Her momentary panic turned into horror as she heard a collision.

Forcing her hand down she stared into the street and watched as Hayden's follow car came to a screeching stop on its roof, pushed into a parked car on the opposite side of the street.

She couldn't see the man in the passenger seat well, but Sloane saw Hayden, still restrained by her seatbelt, upside down and her arms hanging beside her head.

She's okay. Please let her be okay. She's stunned. She's only stunned.

Sloane kept up her rambling thoughts as she and Pilar rushed into the street. She heard Pilar on her phone calling for the EMTs and other law enforcement assistance.

Getting down on her knees, Sloane approached the car and tried to reach in through a broken window.

She felt a scratch along her arm, but that was the least of her worries. "Hayden?"

The deputy was out.

"Damn it, Hayden... you promised your husband!" Sloane reached further and managed to get her fingers along the side of Hayden's neck. A little more of a stretch and she felt a faint, but steady pulse. "She's alive!"

Turning slightly, she was reaching for the passenger when she heard a vehicle slam on its breaks behind her she let out a sigh of relief. "Help's here, guys. I-"

"Sloane, run!"

She heard the rough bark of command in Pilar's voice and her first instinct was to obey, but the instant she stood up, she heard the rolling scrape of a side door.

Sloane turned back and saw Pilar struggling with one

man and another rounding the side of the van heading toward the struggle. She ran straight into the fray.

❧

The world had erupted into chaos. Vicente, Cruz, and the Director were all on their phones. The Director had two calls going, switching back and forth, looking for answers and solutions at the same time.

Vicente was back and forth for a few minutes and then sent a message out to all of the groups on the sting. Four groups answered right away, the last one… ominously silent.

Two groups headed for the blast to discover its source and provide assistance, the other two were sent to the last location for the remaining group. The one including his sister.

❧

The two men managed to toss Pilar into the van, but not without a price.

One man was nearly doubled over from a well-placed mule-kick and the other had lost his mask and a few tracts of skin across his face when Sloane attacked him from behind.

Sloane didn't give up, pushing forward as she dropped the mask to the ground.

For a second, she regretted wearing her flats. If she'd had a heel, she could have done more damage when she nailed him in the back of the knee to stop him from crawling into the van.

He turned around and grabbed a hold of Sloane's arm with one hand, pulling the other back in a fist.

She focused her eyes on his face. If she was going to take the punch, she was going to have some useful information to go with it, but her 'badass' only lasted so long. As his fist descended toward her face, she flinched and found herself untouched by the blow.

"Take the King woman."

Pilar planted an elbow in the side of the man holding her, but that only made him grip her harder, making her wince.

Sloane felt the man lift her off the ground, his arms holding her like iron bands, trapping her arms between them. All she could do as he turned toward the van was kick. She managed to stumble him once, but her victory was short and painful.

He knocked his forehead into hers and the world went black.

❧

With all the emergency personnel descending on the area, it made sense for Vicente to travel on foot. There were already two groups at the scene and two ambulances there as well. It also gave him alternative excuses for the rough scratch in his throat and the thundering rhythm of his heart as he arrived there.

He took a moment to catch his breath and get the lay of the land.

The EMTs were working on Deputy Hatcher and Agent Langston.

Langston looked like he took the worst of the hit. The deputy was conscious and cradling her arm to her chest. Awake was good, for now.

Agent Chu and Deputy Hardwicke jogged over to him with their reports.

"Deputy Bravo and Miss King were both taken-"

"King?" Vicente turned on the Agent with a hard look. "Sloane?"

The two LEOs exchanged looks before Agent Chu continued to speak. "The dash cam shows Miss King with your sister when the van pulled up."

Deputy Hardwicke took up the narrative. "Both of them fought with the men. They grabbed your sister first, but both ladies made sure they had to work for it. At one point Miss King pulled the mask off one of the men."

Vicente started to speak but Agent Chu cut in.

"We already called in to have TARU to use their facial recognition software to get a name on the assailant."

Vicente nodded. He didn't mind the interruption if it cut to the chase. "And the vehicle?"

Apparently, Hardwicke had drawn the short straw.

"Gone. There's a serious lack of security cameras in this neighborhood."

"I bet they've mapped out routes that don't put them past any cameras at all. These men aren't just smart, they're experienced."

Chu continued. "TARU is putting a trace on both women's cell phones. We're waiting to hear back now."

❧

Sloane was only beginning to regain consciousness when the van stopped and the door scraped open. When someone picked her up, she bit into her lip to keep from making a sound. She knew they were in deep trouble and the least she could do was keep her head together even though her heart was pounding like a drumline in her chest.

The only positive thing in their favor was that Pilar Bravo was pissed and swearing in fairly colorful Spanish. If they hadn't been in the middle of hell, she would have asked Pilar to clarify a few of her phrases.

While Sloane had learned and used a fair amount of

Spanish language in her life, the majority of it had come out of 'conversational' textbooks. Some of Pilar's vocabulary was way beyond her knowledge.

She felt the change in her captor's body and did her best to remain limp when he set her down. It wasn't until her head hit the ground that she groaned.

So much for being badass.

"Looks like you didn't hit her too hard."

Sloane opened her eyes and saw one of the men approaching the van, carefully. He was just another man in a mask, but he seemed bulky enough to carry a lot of muscle. She watched as Pilar let the man help her up onto her feet.

Pilar watched him carefully, looking at him from head to toe as if she could somehow decipher his identity from looking at him. She was likely measuring his height and weight and other pertinent facts.

It gave Sloane a little time to gather her nerves. She was dangerously close to sobbing for no other reason than she'd done something that might be epically stupid.

And there was more than a chance… likely a sure thing… that she'd never see Vicente again. Never tell him that she really wanted more with him.

That she was willing to put her heart on the line for him.

That if she had the chance she'd hold on tight to what they had, because she was tired of being closed off to love.

When they sat Pilar down on the floor beside her, Sloane sat up and squeezed she eyes shut for a moment to stave off the vertigo, but it didn't help much.

Pilar sent her a sideways look but didn't speak to her.

That was completely fine with Sloane who seemed to hear even the silence in aching stereo.

Pulling off his hood, the man who originally grabbed Pilar straddled a chair and looked at them. "No hysterics? No begging? Pleading?" He laughed and the stocky man joined in, but the third, the man Sloane had a scratched, remained silent as he pressed a cloth to his cheek.

Sloane took her cue from Pilar.

While she was sure there was no rule book for *Kidnapees* issued by the San Antonio Police Department, she figured that Pilar should run this particular show.

The man straddling the chair folded his arms on the top and gave them both a slow look. “Interesting.”

The injured man chose that moment to break his silence. “He knows they’re here, right?”

His compatriot’s glare said he didn’t like the interruption. “He knows.”

The third man, just barely a foot taller than his sitting friend, stalked over to lean on the table a few feet behind the chair. “Why’d you take off your mask. You know he ain’t gonna like that.”

“He,” spat the man in the chair, “is just going to have to deal with it. Besides, it doesn’t really matter. Does it, Miss Bravo?”

Even bound with her hands behind her, Pilar didn’t give an inch. She glared at the man with her eyes, but her lips curled into a smile.

“Smart woman, aren’t you?”

Sloane looked over at Pilar and saw the steely determination in her eyes and the strong line of her jaw. She saw so much of Vicente’s strength and reticence in that moment that it gave her a taste of hope even as she understood the hidden meaning in the man’s words.

Her eyes turned to look at him and she saw his own knowing smile.

“So the princess gets it.”

Sloane nodded and sat up a little straighter.

The man in the mask was curious. “What are you doing?”

"Mind your own business, go fix your face. You were ugly enough before."

He turned on Sloane, lowering the cloth that he'd pressed to his cheek. The scratch closest to his nose started to bleed freely.

"Bitch. You're going to pay for this before I put a bullet in your head."

"Now, I don't recall giving you any such instructions, Thomas."

They all turned toward the new voice, but Sloane would have bet money that the only person who didn't know who the voice belonged to was Pilar.

"Hello, Uncle Glen."

"My dear niece, I'd like to say I'm shocked to see you." He sighed and stepped inside the building with a ridiculously happy grin on his face. "But then again, you always seem to be exactly where you shouldn't. And sticking your nose in the same places."

As he strode into the room with a man on either side, Sloane saw more of where they were being held.

She'd been in enough old abandoned buildings to know that they were in the old industrial section of town. She'd sold off quite a few buildings to get funds for her foundation, so she'd probably driven by this very building a time or two.

"Go ahead," he gestured at the nearly empty room, "try to figure it out. It doesn't matter either way. No one's going to help you."

Sloane nodded and gave him her own smile.

Why was she poking the bear?

Well, when you had nothing left to lose, what's a little grizzly baiting between family?

"You're right, Uncle, but I'm not the same person anymore."

"Really?" His tone was full of laughter. "Then what are

you? You were a mouse… now… a kitty cat? Thomas' face shows that much."

"Don't mock me," Thomas' expression darkened.

"If you can't protect yourself," her uncle answered back, "don't expect me to defend you."

With a gesture, her uncle called up a man with a heavy leather briefcase.

"So, why don't we get things started."

"Get what started?" Pilar spoke up, easing herself closer to Sloane.

"Nothing to do with you, deputy. You were only going to be bait for Sloane." He looked at the man sitting in the chair, who got up under Glen McKinnon's glare. "You could have just left her behind if you had Sloane."

The man shrugged. "She saw my face," he admitted, "and you never know when you'll need a human shield with things like this." He got up from his chair in the way a cowboy swung his leg to dismount from a horse. "And if there's time, I wouldn't mind a little up-close and personal time to see how rough she likes it."

"You touch me again," Pilar hissed at him, "and you'll have to count on your fingers and toes to get to ten."

He gave her uncle a big smile. "Let me have her and you don't have to pay me."

Glen shrugged. "When I'm done, Alan." He gestured to the table. "Sloane should know that if she fails to sign the contracts that she won't be the one to suffer."

Pilar swore under her breath. "He's supposed to be your uncle?"

Glen pulled the chair away from the table, dragging the legs on the concrete. The din drilled through Sloane's head. "It's an honorary title."

"Honor, my ass."

Standing off to the side, Alan winked at her. "If that's an invitation..."

"Don't goad him on." Sloane turned to Pilar with a harsh tone in her voice. She saw Pilar's confusion written plainly on her face but continued on. She needed just a little bit of time. Curling into herself, Sloane folded her arms around herself and managed to dislodge the burner phone from her bra. "I can't believe we're in this mess."

She could feel Pilar watching her, but she couldn't explain, not right then. She just had to hope that Pilar would catch on. There would be one window of opportunity.

And she had to make sure they could take advantage of it.

❧

The marked SAPD SUV with lights on pushed through the crowd and a call on Vicente's radio pushed him in the car's direction. Before it stopped completely the back-passenger door opened and Sloane's friend, Hildie, jumped out and she rushed toward Vicente.

"Have you found her?"

"Not yet, but we will." Vicente took her by the arm and started walking her toward her car. "We found your car on the street. So, we know she brought it here. We popped the locks, I'm sorry."

"Oh, goodness, do whatever you have to. I'm just sorry I didn't know she'd taken it and then I didn't know what to do."

"Don't worry," he said the words even as his inside twisted even tighter. "We need all the information we can pull together as fast as we can get it. I need you to look in the car and tell me if she took anything with her."

Nodding, Hildie started over to her car, a uniformed officer following her the short distance. He wasn't going to lose anyone else. He had half a mind to follow her but he saw a familiar face come out of the crowd.

"Hey, Bravo, I think I found something you need." Texas Ranger Daxton Chambers held out an evidence bag.

Before he took hold of it he knew what it was. "Pilar's phone."

Daxton nodded. "Screen is smashed. I'd say it was the heel of someone's shoe. It was in the street. I've got others searching, but I think you know what we'll find."

Vicente registered the hard lines of Daxton's face and the set of his jaw. "They'll have dumped Sloane's phone somewhere too."

Biting into his bottom lip, Vicente swore a blue streak in his head.

He felt Daxton's hand clamp down on his shoulder. "Hey… listen to me."

Vicente looked up at his old friend.

"Don't borrow trouble. Men like us," he gave Vicente a smile, "we don't fall for weak women. We fall for the women we don't deserve, women who are far too resourceful for our own peace of mind."

Vicente gave him a hard look. "Fall for? What makes you think I've fallen for Sloane?"

Daxton gave him a smile. "I'd recognize that look anywhere. When I fell, I fell hard and it took me awhile to make sense of it, but it's written plainly on your face if people know what to look for."

Vicente couldn't talk about that, not right then. He had to focus on what happened to her first. "Why did Sloane come down here? She put herself in danger. When I find her-"

"There!" Daxton gave his shoulder a squeeze. "That's the mindset you need to have."

Vicente nodded in return but could only force his words

through clenched teeth. "Even if I've half a mind to throttle the woman when I find her?"

Daxton shook his head. "I'm thinking you should probably stick to reading her the riot act and then make up sex. Much more fun."

Vicente felt a good portion of his anxiety ease up for just a moment, and that cleared his mind, sharpened his focus. "Thanks, Dax, I needed that."

And the Ranger agreed. "Now let's focus on finding them."

"Here, here!" Hildie pushed her way through the group with the officer struggling to keep up. Even in her stylish heels, Hildie could move like a linebacker when she needed to. "I found something."

Vicente met her a few steps away. "What do you have?"

"It's what I don't have," she told him. Holding up the box she gestured to the two charging stations and the one remaining phone. "We give these to women in difficult situations. When their relationships get beyond their own abilities to handle them, we give them these phones. When we move them around from shelter to sanctuary houses, they take this phone with them. Their abusive family member or spouse doesn't know about the phone so they can safely communicate with us and other helpers in the community. I had two phones in here."

Vicente grabbed onto the hope in her voice. "You think she took the other phone."

Hildie shoved the box into the officer's hands and grabbed the front of Vicente's shirt with her hands. "I know she did. Sloane's running on fear and instinct right now. Whatever made her come down here looking for your sister is from her gut. The same gut that she didn't follow the night Kimberly died."

"Her sister?" The question came from Daxton. "What does that have to do with-"

"She had a feeling that something horrible was going to happen to her sister, but her uncle told her she was just over reacting. She didn't go to see her sister that night and a few days later, Kimberly was found dead.

"I think she had the same feeling about your sister today. She was on edge, more so than usual. I think she came here to help Pilar. I'm sure she took the phone."

Digging into her pocket, Hildie pulled her own cell phone out of her pocket and opened the app with phone numbers in it. "Here," she handed the phone over to Vicente, pointing out the number at the bottom of the list. "Track that number. I think you'll find her."

Vicente nodded. "We had officers out looking to find Sloane's phone. The men dumped Pilar's phone on the street."

The officer standing beside Hildie shrugged. "If they took the phones from the women, how did Miss King expect to keep hold of the other cell? Wouldn't they search her just in case?"

Hildie stared down the officer, her chin lifted in indignant anger. "You have no idea where women hide things, do you? Unless these guys get all up close and personal with my girl, they'll miss the phone." She turned back to Vicente.

He was already calling the TARU office. "Trace this number."

CHAPTER 15

They'd been close enough on the floor that when the phone fell out of the bottom of Sloane's oversized sweater it barely made a noise, sliding from the fabric to the floor.

And when Sloane got to her feet, trembling with fear, she managed to shush the phone over to Pilar, to where it was nestled against her leg on the far side from the prying eyes of her uncle and his men.

"I'll sign," she told him and watched as his immediate smile faltered a bit. "I just don't want this to keep coming between us."

She hesitated a few steps away from the table and looked Glen straight in the eye. "I've been fighting you so long on this, I just didn't realize what it was doing to our relationship." Meek and mild, she told herself. Be meek and mild.

He didn't speak. He just stood there by the table, waiting.

She looked at the men that had come after them. The men that had picked them up off the street and thrown them both in the van. They watched her too, and she couldn't help but feel like they were staring at her like prey.

Sloane supposed she was. After all, they had all the

advantages. They had weapons and numbers and muscle.

But what they didn't have was a need to get home like she did.

So, when Sloane took a seat at the table, she did everything she could to keep their eyes on her.

She didn't want to give them a reason to hurt Pilar. Not now. Not like this.

The man with the briefcase set a pen down on the table. "Miss King. Would you like me to explain what's in the documents?"

Her first instinct was to tell him no, that she'd sign no matter what it said. The last thing she cared about in that moment was money or her inheritance. Lives were at stake.

But she knew, just like Pilar did, that once the papers were signed, once she'd done everything her uncle- everything that Glen wanted, they would just get rid of her and Pilar too. Two of them had lost their masks and they'd both seen Glen. If they were set free, they could testify against him.

And Glen may have been a jerk of an uncle, but he knew how to level companies and men's legacies.

What would he care about two women in the grand scheme of things?

Without looking at Glen, she could see the gleam in his eye. He didn't care for her one bit. He'd likely never cared about her.

She had to give Vicente time to come to them. Even if Pilar had her hands available, they outnumbered three to one, and only the other side had weapons.

"Miss King?"

Startled out of her thoughts, she tried to keep the pliant look of confusion on her face. There seemed to be hundreds of tabs on the sides of the documents. That would keep her busy for awhile.

"No, I'll sign. Just show me where." She picked up the first of the many thick document folders. "Let's start with this one."

As he began to explain she noticed the man reaching into his briefcase. She tensed hoping that this wasn't a ruse on their part and he wasn't about to shoot her right there. Instead he withdrew a leather-bound volume and an embosser.

The lawyer was also a notary.

Just great.

When her uncle decided to put the screws to her he didn't miss a thing.

❧

Cruz rushed over and shoved a tablet into Vicente's hands. "Here. It's from TARU."

Vicente stared at the image before him and held onto it like a lifeline.

"We've got cars ready and everyone's in on this."

It took a real effort not to run blindly into the street and grab the first car he came to. Keys? Who needed keys at a time like this.

He followed Cruz and the two of them climbed into the back of a department-issued SUV and started to pull on their Kevlar vests. The vehicle pulled away from the curb and Vicente looked over at Cruz. "You've got the plan?"

Cruz nodded slowly. "I know this is tough for you, letting me take the lead."

Vicente looked up as he fastened the side flaps of his vest. "Not tough at all." He let go of a pent-up breath. "You're the one I want to plan this. I'm too close." He leaned his head back and stared at the ceiling of the car. "Sloane and my sister? My heart is going a million miles an hour, my blood pressure is a degree under boiling. I'd be ready to walk us into an ambush to get them back."

"And we'll get them back."

"I know." Vicente held out his hand to his friend. "I know you'll make it happen. I just want to be there to see these men go down for this."

Cruz reached out and grabbed his friend's forearm and Vicente mirrored the hold. "We'll get them back, my friend. I'm going to do everything I can. You'd do the same for me."

"Any day," Vicente agreed with his friend, "every day."

They shook on it and Cruz gave Vicente's arm a reassuring squeeze. "And twice on Sunday."

The driver turned back to speak. "We're two minutes out."

Cruz leaned forward leaning his arm against the back of the shotgun seat. "Headlights off."

The lights in front of the SUV shuttered and they continued by the moonlight and whatever ambient light they could catch. The Com in Vicente's ear flared to life and he heard Cruz in stereo.

"Everyone has their assignments?"

All the groups replied to the affirmative.

"EMTs standing by." More replies.

"First Priority is the recovery of the victims. Second is neutralizing the threat."

Another voice came onto the line. It only took a second to recognize Hayden. "I'll be with all of you in spirit, but I'm thinking by the time you get there, Pilar will have all of them hogtied and begging for mercy."

Vicente couldn't help the smug smile that tugged at his lips. "Then we'll be there to clean up after her. Thanks, Hayden. Take care of yourself."

"We'll be fine, Bravo. Now go bring my friends home."

"Yes, ma'am."

❧

Sloane looked at the documents and picked up the pen in her hand. Biting into her lower lip she turned to look at the man she'd wanted to be close to. She saw the venom in his eyes and seething anger just beneath the surface.

How she'd missed it before, she just didn't know.

She'd missed so much.

What had she missed with Kimberly?

She set the pen down and set her hand over it. "Let Pilar go."

The room which had already seemed too quiet by half went as silent as the grave.

Every head in the room turned to Glen McKinnon and waited.

The silence stretched on until it felt like a cramp, tightening by degrees.

Sloane felt like she was walking the line between dread and the slightest bit of irrational hope.

Until the man who she'd thought of as family walked right up to the table where she was sitting, planted his hands on the top of the table, and leaned down into her face.

"Do you have any idea what you've stuck your prissy little nose into?"

She didn't speak. She didn't dare.

She'd seen that look before, just not directed at her, and now it chilled her to the bone.

"I've made a pretty penny selling off bitches like you."

Sloane felt the color drain from her face and all she could do was blink, as stunned as she was.

"Imagine my surprise," he smiled at her and she waited for him to bare his teeth like the jackal he was, "when my philanthropic little niece decided to spend her time and her family's money trying to save the same worthless people that I was using as merchandise. You've always been a thorn in my side.

"I thought after your parents died, you've be as easy to control as your sister. You were the youngest. But you were the most willful child. Why Kimberly tried to protect you, I just don't know."

"Kimberly?" Sloane stood and set a hand on the table top as she swayed, a little dizzy. "What are you talking about?"

"Your sister was... a good girl. She did everything I asked of her. And when I was going to punish you for misbehaving, she took your punishment.

"Who knows," he shrugged, a throwaway of movement that made her stomach turn, "she might have lived longer if you hadn't worn her down."

Sloane moved closer. "What are you talking about?"

"Sloane, stay back."

She heard Pilar's warning, but she couldn't listen, not now.

"What do you know? What happened to Kimberly?"

"Sloane, stop!"

Her feet planted on the concrete, but she kept her focus on her uncle, less than a foot away. "Tell me."

"She took pills to dull the pain." His words were short, pointed, and jabbed like a stick. "But she took what I gave her and thanked me for it."

Sloane lifted a hand to her throat, trying to quell the turmoil roiling in her gut.

"And when you'd mouth off to me, she'd take even more, smiling through the pain because she knew how much it pissed me off.

"Your sister became my personal whipping post to save your hide."

Bile rose in Sloane's throat and she barely kept it in.

"You're a monster."

"You're the one that made her suffer. When you told Kimberly you didn't want to live with me, she got me to agree to let you go."

Sloane's vision started to darken at the edges.

"You're remembering now, aren't you? Those nights she spent at my house? The long weekends? That was all in payment for your willful behavior, little girl."

Her knees went weak and her heart stuttered in her chest. "No. No. She would have told me."

"Really?" His laughter rang off the walls. "Remember who had control of the estate? That was me, baby. I owned the both of you. She wasn't going to say a thing, because if she told..."

Everything went to hell a moment later. The doors on both sides of the building burst inward and suddenly the air was filled with noise.

She couldn't hear much more than the rush of blood through her ears, but she managed to raise her head and see that the men around her were standing, stock still, their guns trained on the people rushing into the room.

FBI, SAPD, RANGER- the bright white letters stamped on their vests read like a Bible verse of salvation, but Sloane couldn't help but think it wasn't over.

Not yet.

Cruz. She heard his voice ring out as the rest of the noise died down. "That's right, fingers off the triggers. Pilar, Sloane, walk to me."

It took a moment for Sloane's brain to register the words and then she had to make her feet move. She still had the weight of his words on her shoulders.

"Sloane."

She heard her name whispered under his breath and she looked up into his face, waiting to hear what he had to say.

"I wanted you to die."

"Sloane," it was Cruz this time, "step away from him."

"I was going to give you a taste of what Kimberly enjoyed for years, and then I was going to let you take your own life like she did."

Her eyes widened ever so slightly, and her heart sped up in her chest. "You're never going to hurt another woman ever again."

His whole expression changed. His eyes changed from stormy to cold and cruel and she realized that he'd heard a challenge in her voice.

It was too late to take it back, but she was almost relieved. She'd heard too much and knew too much to play the good girl for him. Not when he'd used her to hurt her sister.

"It would be so easy to kill you, but then it would be over for you."

"Damn it, Sloane, walk away from him!"

Pilar's tone turned her head.

"But this will be more fun."

Just as she started to move, she saw him reach into his coat. By the time she saw the butt of a gun in his hand she knew she wasn't going to be the target. He wanted her alive. He wanted her suffering.

And there was one visible target in the room that he could get to.

The only other person not protected by a Kevlar vest.

"No." Sloane threw herself against him as he tried to extend his arm to fire. Wrapping her arm around his she pulled it down toward the ground as he tried to push her away.

Her ears rang again as several shots rang out.

A moment later she was falling. When she came to a stop, she was sprawled on the ground, halfway under her uncle, and blood soaking through her clothes.

❧

Vicente reached Sloane's side at the same time Pilar did. Together they lifted Glen McKinnon off of her and rolled him onto his back, still breathing, but gushing blood.

He didn't care if someone tried to save the man's life, he had more important things to do.

He had to save someone more important than anything else.

He felt Sloane's eyes on him as he pulled apart her blouse and smoothed his fingers through the blood on her skin. "Are you hurt, Sloane?"

She lay still beneath his hands.

"Damn it, Sloane, are you hurt?"

He felt her hand touch his cheek and he looked up.

Her soft green eyes looked into his. She was near tears, her lashes glittering with some untold emotion. "I don't think it's my blood."

Vicente heard the wooden tone of her voice, the syllables thick on her tongue. And from his side, he heard the words that he already had in his head.

"She's in shock."

Pilar touched his shoulder with her hand. "I'll get the EMTs in here. Stay with her."

He wasn't going anywhere.

Vicente moved up, closer to her head, putting a restraining hand on her shoulder when she tried to get up. "Stay still, baby."

She tried again.

"Hey… I'm not joking. Let them check you out first."

"I," she closed her mouth and bit into her lower lip so hard that the pale line that showed around her teeth was starting to turn pink, "I don't know how much you heard."

Getting up on his knees he touched his hand to the side of her face and leaned over so he was all she could see. "I don't care what he said. I care that he hurt you. I care that he was trying to make you suffer.

"And I care that I wasn't able to get here any sooner."

She nodded, an odd rocking movement dictated by the hard floor under her. "Hildie?"

He smiled. "You are, without a doubt, the most frustrating woman I've ever met."

She tensed and her skin paled, letting him know that he'd unknowingly hit a little too close to home.

He wiped his hands off on his slacks and found her hand, drawing it up between them so he could place it against his chest, palm first.

Vicente watched as the tension eased from her body.

"You need to know something, Sloane."

Her eyes fixed on his, a mix of emotions turned her soft green eyes into a dark stormy sea.

"I love you." He held her hand to him with both hands, feeling the harsh beat of his heart and the warmth of her hand against the same thin wall of flesh. "And I'm going to love you forever. That's what I was thinking tonight before we even started the operation. You're it for me."

He watched as she swallowed, and a tear slipped out of the corner of her eye and into her hair.

He heard the wheels of a gurney rattling in through the door.

"I just want you to remember that while they're taking a look at you. Just hold onto that thought, Sloane, until you can hold onto me."

She nodded and then he felt a touch on his arm.

"Agent Bravo, please step back."

He gave her hand a squeeze and then set it gently down at her side before he got to his feet and moved away.

CHAPTER 16

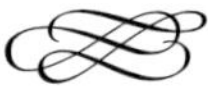

When Sloane was released from the hospital just before dawn, Vicente walked her to the Departmental SUV and helped her inside even though they both knew she didn't need the help. They just couldn't seem to stop touching each other.

Hands clasped, or fingers entwined.

He'd smoothed his hand over her back while they'd waited for her x-rays. She leaned against his shoulder when Pilar had come to visit after she was released almost an hour before.

They touched to reassure, and they touched to soothe. All of it was just another affirmation that they'd both made it through the last night alive and breathing.

After he closed her door and made his way around to the driver's side, they sat in their seats for a long silent moment.

Neither spoke.

Neither seemed to move.

But there was nothing difficult or strained about the distance between them. It just was.

"Are you," her voice seemed to startle them both, "are you going to go home after you drop me off at my apartment?"

He turned to answer her, but she was looking straight out of the windshield, her hands folded in her lap. Vicente smiled as she blew out a breath between her slightly parted lips.

"I was hoping you'd come to my place."

She turned to look at him, her eyes widening. "Your place?"

He shrugged. I know I've been a bachelor for a long time, but if there's one thing our mother drilled into our heads, especially the boys, was that we had two hands just like everyone else so we could clean.

"So, unless someone broke in while I was gone, it should be clean enough for human habitation."

She shook her head and he felt a knot twist his stomach.

"I'm not worried about how clean it is," she told him. "I just want to make sure that it's what you want."

"Sloane-"

"No, let me say this."

He heard the plea in her voice and nodded. "Okay."

Turning on the seat, she met his gaze evenly and let out a breath. "When we were in the warehouse, you told me you loved me and it was the most beautiful thing I've ever heard. Just moments before I was sure that I was going to die and that your sister would too. I couldn't stand the thought that you'd lose someone you loved because of me.

"And then, you were there, telling me everything was going to be okay. You weren't angry at me. You didn't blame me. You told me you loved me. And I knew everything was going to be just fine.

"So, if you want me to go to your place, then let's go, because once we get inside and I can get you alone, I'm going to show you how much you mean to me, Vicente." She leaned closer and traced her fingertips down the side of his face and down to his shoulder. "Because I love you too."

Smiling, he turned back to the steering wheel and started the SUV. He backed out of the parking spot, but before he changed the gear to drive he gave her a pointed look. "I never said I wasn't angry, Sloane. You scared me. Terrified me. I wish I'd known what you were doing, but we're not going to talk about it today."

He shifted gears and they started forward, heading to the exit.

"Then when are we going to talk about it?"

He heard the hesitation in her voice and knew he wasn't going to drag it out. "Later. Tomorrow. Sooner the better. We're going to have a talk about and we'll likely argue about it, but I'm told that make up sex is something we shouldn't miss. We can do that tomorrow too."

She laughed as the SUV bumped down onto the main road outside the hospital.

❧

If you asked her later what the outside of Vicente's house looked like, she wouldn't have a clue. Every cell of her body was focused on keeping her hands to her herself until they were inside.

When the SUV was put into Park, she had her seatbelt undone and the door open. They two set foot on the ground at the same time and before he could come around to get her, she met him at the front of the vehicle.

He took her hand in his and they made their way up the path to the porch. That was all she could remember. A porch. A door. And then the lock clicking into place with a resounding click. When he finished setting the alarm he turned toward her. "Do you want me to show you around or-"

Her hands grasped the front of his shirt and pulled it open, sending at least one button flying.

She saw the curious look in his eyes, but she also saw the way his lips parted. She knew those lips.

Knew what they felt like on her skin, but she also knew it meant he was trying to slow his breathing… trying to control his need. Vicente liked to touch and taste, but he was willing to let her take control and it only made her hungrier for him.

"It's only fair," she told him as she pushed his shirt off his shoulders, "you ruined my shirt."

They both knew it was a lie. All the blood that had soaked into her shirt had ruined it, but neither of them wanted to think about that. She was sure of it.

The shirt fell but didn't fall from his hands.

He tugged them apart and cleared his throat as she reached for his belt.

"I'm busy," she told him as she released the buckle and made quick work of pulling the end free.

"I think you forgot my cuffs," she heard the note of amusement in his voice.

"Cuffs," she repeated, "what a perfect name for them."

When she pulled his zipper down in one quick movement he hissed slightly.

"Careful," he cautioned her, "don't want to catch something down there."

"Oh, I don't, do I?"

Before he could answer, she slipped her hand into the waistband of his boxer-briefs and wrapped her hand around his thickening length.

"You want me to let it go?"

As she eased his pants down onto his hips she looked up and saw the way his eyes had darkened, and when she drew her closed hand up from the base of his cock to the head she saw him lick his bottom lip before pulling it between his teeth.

"Or," she wondered as she got down on her knees on his carpet, "do you want me to keep going?"

His eyes lowered and she knew what he could see, her pale hand wrapped around his shaft and bumping up against the head.

"Well, I guess that's a-" she took him into her mouth, chasing her hand as it lowered to the base.

"Yes." He groaned and she felt his hips push forward. "That's a yes..."

She couldn't help the surge of heat that traced through her veins at the feeling of him in her mouth. The power she felt holding him in her hand. It was a heady sensation, but it felt so good to give him this gift.

She explored his length with her gentle fist and the flat of her tongue. The ridges and velvety skin felt like heaven, and the deeper she took him, the more his head rubbed at the top of her mouth, near the back of her soft palate. The sensations were subtle but seemed to tickle her throat with his touch.

As she moved back, he rocked back on his feet and stumbled back against the door.

"Baby," his voice crawled out of his throat and she heard a series of soft noises against the door, "I want to touch you."

She pulled back, releasing him from her mouth with a soft pop. "Wait your turn." She sat back on her heels and looked up into his face.

His eyes were dark with want, the lines of his face, tight and angular, giving his face an appearance more suited to an animal on the hunt than a human.

"You'll get your chance to play. Let me have my fun." And just to show him how much she was enjoying it, she held him gently at the base of his erection and leaned forward. When she was just an inch away from him she let her tongue peak out from between her lips.

She heard him suck in a breath and when she turned ever so slightly to the side, she saw his eyes fixed on her.

As she touched the tip of her tongue to the underside of his cock it twitched in her hand and a grunt kicked through his body.

A slow litany of words poured from his lips and when she swirled her tongue around the smooth dome of his head she felt his hips push forward and his balls tightened up, brushing against the backs of her fingers.

She looked up and saw his face pulled tight and his forehead furrowed as she felt his muscles tensing.

"You're going to have to tell me what you said later," she smiled when he managed to open his eyes wide enough to look down at her, "I have a lot to learn if we're going to be together."

A shudder passed through him as she leaned forward again and dipped her tongue into the opening on the tip and pulled the pearl of pre-cum into her mouth.

"If you get any better at this, I'm going to lose my mind." His eyes slid closed as her hand drew up along his length.

"I think I'm going to like that challenge," she told him, "I want to make you happy."

"You already do, Sloane. Just by loving me." He tried to lift his hand to touch her and growled as he lowered his hand back against the door. "When are you going to let me have my hands back?"

She considered his words for a moment and then she shrugged. "You know," she gave him a wink, "I didn't think it through." Getting up to her feet she reached to his side and tugged on the sleeve only to find that it was good and stuck on his wrist. "You want me to pull it back up and-"

He'd leaned forward and reached over with his fingers,

slipping them between his skin and the cuff. A good tug and a low tearing sound reached her ears.

"I could have gotten you a pair of scissors, or-"

He brought his hands around front and rid himself of the other cuff.

"Now that was just wasteful."

"Really?" He raised an eyebrow at her. He pushed his pants and underwear down to the floor and toed off his shoes, leaving him naked before her. "The real waste is that I'm naked, and you're not."

"How do you suggest that we remedy this situation, Agent Bravo?"

He took one step closer, completely at ease with her. "You've got two choices, Miss King."

She couldn't help the smile that lifted the corners of her mouth.

"You can strip down right here, and I put you up on my counter and christen the first room of my house, or you make a run for it and I get to have you wherever I catch you."

She considered the options even as her body caught fire at the look in his eyes and the promise in his words.

"Well, neither one has a downside really, but why waste the energy of running away from you," she stepped closer and felt a rush of liquid heat between her thighs, "when I'd rather have you inside me."

Just to prove her point she reached down and pulled the hem of her borrowed scrubs up and over her head.

With her other clothes in evidence, all she was left with was her scrub bottoms.

"Take them off, Sloane."

His voice was low and thick with his arousal and just hearing her name on his lips made her ache to feel him inside of her again.

She met his gaze with her own hungry need and it took

all of a few seconds to hook her fingers and drop the pale blue pants to the ground at her feet.

She reached down and pushed her flats off her heels, and when she looked back up she saw him inches from her.

His arms wrapped around her and his hands slid back and over the curve of her ass. He grabbed hold and lifted her from the floor.

It was only a moment before she felt the cool granite of his countertop under her. The shock of the colder temperature had her leaning forward and put her bare breasts on display.

"I have to say that I like what the cold did to you." Vicente lifted a fingertip and brushed it over her nipple, watching as even his lightest touch drew her flesh tight. "And I love what my touch does to you."

"'*Cente,* I- oh!"

He swept his tongue across her nipple and then back in the other direction. She couldn't help the breathy moan that fell from her lips, but the arch she put in her back, the way she braced her palms against the granite counter top? That was all her.

Sloane wanted to enjoy the view and enjoy she did.

While he took the tip of one breast in his mouth, he continued to brush his fingers over the crest of the other.

One breast warm and wet, the other teased by his skin, instinct and need for him, arched her back even more, pressing her breast deeper into his mouth where he could taste and tempt with the rough scratch of his tongue.

When he switched and wrapped his lips around the beaded nipple of her other breast she felt a rush of warmth between her legs and the gasp from her lips was followed by a moan. It sounded like a purr deep in her throat and when she managed to look down at him, his eyes were watching her with triumph in his gaze.

Bracing his hands on either side of her hips, Vicente leaned in closer and licked the plumped flesh of her bottom lip. "Keep biting on it and you're going to draw blood, and I've had enough of you being in the hospital to last me a lifetime."

He paused, his eyes moving over her face and then slowly down her body. Moving his feet the slightest bit he drew closer to her body using his hips to move her legs further out to the side, nestling against her. Lifting his hand, he placed his palm on her belly, brushing over her skin around her belly button. "But one day," he murmured low as his other hand joined the first, mirroring his touch on the other side of her body, "when you're round and full with our child, I'm going to be there beside you waiting for our baby to take its first breath. That's the only need you'll have for a hospital from now on."

She wanted to tell him that you couldn't just will things like that into being, but she felt the warmth of his touch, saw the reverence of his expression as he touched her body and wondered if things couldn't just be that simple.

"Our child? Just one?"

His eyes rose up and met her in challenge. "At a time. I don't think I could handle more than one at a time. I'll be a big enough mess as it is." His breaths came shorter as he touched her, their eyes searching each other's. And when she was sure she was ready to fall into his arms and beg him to give her more, she felt his fingers between her legs.

Felt him slide a finger between her folds, teasing her with its slow, delicious stroke.

She edged forward, her legs spreading just the littlest bit wider. "More."

He smiled and a second finger joined the first, pushing just a little deeper until she was sure that he'd worked his fingers in to his first knuckle.

She shook her head. "More, Vicente. I want you inside me."

With a smile against her lips, he slipped his tongue into her mouth. She gasped and parted her lips to give him whatever access he wanted.

When his tongue stroked against hers, she felt him sink two fingers deep into her core.

Her lower back arched and he went deeper as her pointed nipples brushed against his chest.

"This?" He murmured the question against the corner of her mouth, working his fingers inside of her. "Or something else?"

She rode his fingers, rocking her hips against him as if she was reaching for something, trying to get just a little closer. "More."

He withdrew his fingers and her eyes flew open, her mouth parting on a huff.

"'*Cente,* that's-"

"Patience, Sloane. Give me a chance and I'll make it worth the wait."

She leaned in and pressed a hard kiss to his lips. "How long?"

He gripped her hips and lifted her from the counter and set her back on her feet. She narrowed her eyes at him, flashing with a playful warning. "I love it when you need me," he smiled at her, but she wasn't quite done with him yet.

Before she could move, he turned her around. Taking one hand off her hips he took hold of one of her hands and set it on the countertop, palms flat on the granite.

When she moved her other hand, matching the position of the first he used his hand to rub the firm flesh of her hip. "I think you see what I want here."

She gave him a look over her shoulder. "Well, I know what I want."

He gave her a questioning look.

"You."

Nodding, he leaned forward and bit the shell of her ear with a playful nip. "Then I think we're both going to be very happy." He nudged one of her feet to the side and she repeated the move with the other.

"Nice to know you can follow instructions."

"Ohh..." she shook her head, "you're going to pay for that later."

He winked and leaned forward, flattening one palm against her belly and the other on her lower back. Vicente bent her over the counter using gentle pressure on her body and when he stopped, he leaned into her ear.

"Quiero sentir tu cuerpo junto al mío," his voice sent a shiver through her body, and the things that his teeth and tongue were doing to the sensitive length of her neck should be illegal... later.

"I wish," she gasped as he placed an open-mouthed kiss on the back of her neck, "that I'd paid more attention in my language class."

She heard the tell-tale rip of a foil packet a moment before he spoke again.

"I doubt they'd teach you that in a class," before she could turn around to look at him, he set his hands on her hips and bit his fingers into her flesh. "Stay still and I'll tell you."

It took a lot of effort to remain still, but she was dying to know what he'd whispered into her ear. As she stood there, he lifted a hand from her skin and a moment later she felt him press up against her folds.

Instinct curved her back, giving him room to press forward. And press forward he did. Once the head of his cock slipped into her body she felt his muscled chest against her back and heard the thick rumble of his voice in her ear.

"I said, 'I want to feel your body next to mine.'"

And then he was in, all the way inside her, his hips pressed flush against her backside and his chest against her back.

She used her hands on the counter and pushed back. "I do love the way you feel against me," she sighed. "I'll have to learn that phrase for later."

"But now," he prompted her as he began to withdraw from her body, "all you have to do…"

She clenched her muscles, trying to hold him inside, but he didn't stop until he was almost free of her heat. "All I have to do?"

She would have sworn she could feel him smiling, if that was even possible.

"All you have to do is hold on."

And then there wasn't time for talking.

He filled her over and over again, sinking deeper if such a thing was possible.

As she leaned against the counter, she went down to her elbows, needing the hard, flat surface to brace against, and that's when she felt the world around her shift.

His arm around her waist, the other braced beside her elbow, he filled her body with each hard stroke and her soul with his body wrapped around hers, his words filling her ears.

When his body pushed her over the edge, she fell apart into an untold number of pieces, but it was his tender care and loving concern that put her back together again, stronger than she was before.

Stronger, because they were together.

EPILOGUE

PILAR

Pilar took the beer that her brother handed her and gave it an absent-minded sip as she took in the gathering around her. Her family, forever an excitable mob, were laughing and dancing. The smaller children playing games in the grass and chasing each other around the clearing.

She had less than an hour before she was scheduled to go to the airport, but the whole San Antonio Bravo branch of their family tree had been celebrating since mid-morning so she'd gotten her fill and then some.

Most of her family didn't understand why she felt the urge to move away. Certainly, they didn't understand why she choose somewhere as far from home as Center City.

Looking up from her beer, she saw Sloane making her way over to her side. It still made her laugh from time to time. Her brother, who came from their staunchly blue-collar background, had met and married a woman from the height from San Antonio society.

And yet it wasn't as odd as it sounded. Sloane certainly

didn't act like a lot of other people in her position. She never minded getting dirty on clean-up duty or in her everyday life.

Pilar has seen Sloane dressed to the nines for a fancy event, looking completely amazing standing next to her brother, who managed to wear a tux without making stupid penguin jokes. And Sloane was equally at home in a crazy ragtag group like her family.

And despite the amazing photos that Pilar had seen of her in the past, Sloane had never looked so beautiful as when they had gathered in her family's small community church, wearing a simple white gown holding an armful of roses moments before she pledged her life and eternal love as Vicente put his ring on her finger and she in turn put her ring on him.

Leaving a small group by one of the picnic tables, Pilar opened her arms to her newest sister and gave Sloane a hug.

"Are you sure you don't want us to take you to the airport?"

Placing a kiss on Sloane's cheek, Pilar stepped back just a tad, looking into her soft green eyes.

"I'm fine. I've got a ride coming to pick me up. You two should stay here and enjoy the picnic."

Vicente stepped up beside his wife and gently pulled her into his side. He placed a gentle kiss on her temple and whispered something in her ear that made her blush.

"What's up with you two?" The secrecy between the two had been evident all day. They were always affectionate with each other, but since they'd arrived at the picnic site to help set up, they'd had these little moments when Pilar could have sworn they were hiding something.

All it took was one pointed look in her brother's direction and she solved the riddle herself.

"How far along?"

The two turned their heads in her direction and stared.

Sloane lifted her hand and set it low on her belly. "About six weeks. We didn't want to make a big announcement yet."

Pilar nodded, the first trimester was a difficult time for some families. "I agree, it's good to wait for the announcement, especially in this family, you'd never get any peace."

Their sister Yolanda had lost two pregnancies in her first trimester, and knowing Sloane the way she did, they were concerned about her reaction.

"Still, I'm glad I know. I'm so happy for both of you!" She gave them both a hug, gathering each of them close, hoping to remember that very moment in the months to come.

When they stepped back, she couldn't help but notice that Vicente's hand had settled on Sloane's belly.

"You're both going to be the most amazing parents."

She turned her gaze to Sloane, wondering how she would take the comment.

When they'd met, Sloane had had such a tough past with her family, she didn't want to remind her of her past.

But again, Sloane surprised her.

Beaming ear to ear, Sloane leaned her head on Vicente's shoulder. "We're going to do everything we can to make sure our baby knows how wanted and loved he is."

"He?" The question came from her brother. "How do you know?"

Sloane smoothed her hand up his forearm and Pilar couldn't help but see the way her touch soothed him.

"I just have a feeling." Sloane shrugged. "Just like I have a feeling that Pilar's move is going to be a good one. And… she knows that we're here for her if she needs anything."

Pilar lifted a hand in a half-hearted gesture of surrender. "Don't I know it. I'm sure if I stub my toe and let you know about it you'll have a whole caravan of cars headed my way straight up through the center of the country."

Vicente let a comical expression of shock widen his eyes and smiled. "I do believe she understands how much we can throw ourselves into our work."

And it was true, Pilar agreed. While Glen McKinnon rotted in the Federal Penitentiary, convicted of enough crimes to keep him in there for two lifetimes, his entire organization had been dismantled and nearly four dozen men were sent to jail for anywhere from ten years to a lifetime in jail, the Helping Hearts Foundation had continued to be a force of change and a dedicated source of comfort for women and children in need.

The entire Alphabet soup of local and federal law enforcement in San Antonio were even more involved in their efforts.

First responders in all areas were volunteering to help those in fear and pain in a more preventative capacity. Citizens all over San Antonio as well as the government at different levels had acknowledged the positive effects of this new partnership.

"I hope you know that when I get settled in Center City, I'll be talking with my commanding officers about your programs."

Seeing Sloane's genuine joy filled Pilar with joy herself. "We do our best here, but Center City… it's several times the size of San Antonio."

Pilar nodded. "True, but every big city is comprised of smaller communities and it's those smaller communities that will need help the most.

"If we can get even a few of the same programs started, tap into First Responders there as we have here, think of all the good we could do for those that need it. Some, more than most."

Sloane stepped forward and pulled Pilar tight into her embrace. Leaning closer, she whispered into her ear. "I love you, Pilar. You're as much my sister as Kimberly was. If I can do anything to help you get your programs started, just let me know."

"And I know," Pilar squeezed her right back, "that you'll take care of things here for me. Keep my brother in line, for one."

Sloane leaned back and gave Pilar a look of pained exhaustion. "I will do my best, but your brother…" she let out a dramatic sigh and pressed the back of her hand to her forehead with a groan, "he may be beyond my help."

Before Pilar could say anything, Vicente swept his wife up into his arms and Sloane wrapped her arms around his neck with a peel of laughter.

Pilar rolled her eyes. "You better not drop her, brother. Mama will smack you with her slipper."

He shrugged and Sloane wrapped her arms tighter around him at the sudden movement. "I've managed to live this long. I will survive whatever Mama throws at me."

Sloane grew still in his arms and he turned to look at his wife. "What, baby? What's wrong?"

Vicente looked at Pilar and she gave him a big wink before waving at him to turn around.

Standing behind him was half the family, centered around their parents.

"What's everyone looking at?"

Their brother, Alejandro, gave him a smug look. "A dead man walking if Mama thinks you've done something bad."

To prove his point, their mother, Claudia, folded her arms across her generous bosom and narrowed her eyes at him.

"Mama?" He shrugged and Sloane laughed again.

"You're going to make me sea sick if you don't stop."

"See?" Alejandro gestured at Vicente. "Go get him, Mama."

Sloane turned to look back at Pilar. "What is she going to do?"

Pilar pursed her lips together, trying to smother her smile.

Alejandro's smug expression disappeared when his mother gave his arm a pinch. "Mama? What the hell!?"

That earned him an open-handed smack on his arm.

"Hey!"

Claudia wagged her finger at the youngest of the Bravos. "Stop trying to cause trouble for Vicente. You should follow his example and marry a good woman."

Alejandro's complexion soured.

Yolanda cuffed her brother on his shoulder. "See what happens when you try to get him in trouble? It ends up squarely on you. Give up now before '*Cente* puts you in a headlock."

The youngest lifted his chin in defiance. "I can take it."

"I know one thing that you won't be able to 'take.'" Setting Sloane gently down on the ground, Vicente ambled toward his brother.

Alejandro stood his ground, his arms straight and stiff at his sides. "You won't get me this time, Vicente," even though he shook the littlest bit as their brother neared him, Alejandro stood his ground. "I'm ready for you."

Vicente stood before his brother with his whole body loose and easy. Without warning or preamble, he grabbed his brother with both hands on his ribs and tickled.

As the assembled group started to pick sides in this epic battle between brothers, Pilar's phone beeped, and she looked at it with a smile. "And that is my cue to leave."

Leaning into Sloane, she gave her friend and sister-in-law one last gentle kiss on her cheek. "You better send me pictures of the belly."

Sloane kissed her right back. "You know I will. Take care

of yourself too. I don't think the Center City Police Department is ready for you. I'm just glad you're ready for them, Pilar. You're destined for good things."

Pilar bent down to pick up her carryon bag. "I already have good things. I have the best family in the world."

Taking one last look at the chaos surrounding her, Pilar Bravo took the first step in the next part of her life.

Looking for the next book in Reina's San Antonio First Responders series? Well, you can get it NOW!!! Justice for Miranda is just one click away!!

ABOUT REINA TORRES

Love - Romance - Books

Aren't they all the same thing?

Oh, I sure hope so!

I've been reading romance books for what seems like forever. When I was a teen, the days that I wasn't in dance class after school I'd go to the mall to wait for my mom to finish work for the day and my haunt of choice... Waldenbooks. (I think I just showed my age there.)

Whether it was Scottish Lairds, Medieval Knights, Regency Gents, Rough and Tumble Cowboys, or handsome modern Heroes, I loved them all! There was always another hero and heroine to follow through page after page of breathless love!

I really hope that my readers will enjoy some of the same thrills as discover characters to love between the pages of my books.

amazon.com/author/reinatorresromance
twitter.com/rtorresauthor
bookbub.com/authors/reina-torres

Jenika Snow: Protecting Lily
Lynne St. James: SEAL's Spitfire
Dee Stewart: Conner
Harley Stone: Rescuing Mercy
Jen Talty: Burning Desire
Reina Torres, Rescuing Hi'ilani
Savvi V: Loving Lex
Megan Vernon: Protecting Us
Rachel Young: Because of Marissa

Delta Team Three Series

Lori Ryan: Nori's Delta
Becca Jameson: Destiny's Delta
Lynne St James, Gwen's Delta
Elle James: Ivy's Delta
Riley Edwards: Hope's Delta

Police and Fire: Operation Alpha World

Freya Barker: Burning for Autumn
BP Beth: Scott
Julia Bright, Justice for Amber
Anna Brooks, Guarding Georgia
KaLyn Cooper: Justice for Gwen
Aspen Drake: Sheltering Emma
Deanndra Hall: Shelter for Sharla
Barb Han: Kace
EM Hayes: Gambling for Ashleigh
CM Steele: Guarding Hope
Reina Torres: Justice for Sloane
Aubree Valentine, Justice for Danielle
Maddie Wade: Finding English
Stacey Wilk: Stage Fright
Laine Vess: Justice for Lauren

Tarpley VFD Series

Silver James, Fighting for Elena
Deanndra Hall, Fighting for Carly
Haven Rose, Fighting for Calliope
MJ Nightingale, Fighting for Jemma
TL Reeve, Fighting for Brittney
Nicole Flockton, Fighting for Nadia

As you know, this book included at least one character from Susan Stoker's books. To check out more, see below.

SEAL of Protection: Legacy Series

Securing Caite
Securing Brenae (novella)
Securing Sidney
Securing Piper
Securing Zoey
Securing Avery
Securing Kalee (Sept 2020)
Securing Jane (Feb 2021)

SEAL Team Hawaii Series

Finding Elodie (Apr 2021)
Finding Lexie (Aug 2021)
Finding Kenna (Oct 2021)
Finding Monica (TBA)
Finding Carly (TBA)
Finding Ashlyn (TBA)

Delta Team Two Series

Shielding Gillian
Shielding Kinley (Aug 2020)
Shielding Aspen (Oct 2020)
Shielding Riley (Jan 2021)
Shielding Devyn (May 2021)
Shielding Ember (Sep 2021)
Shielding Sierra (TBA)

Delta Force Heroes Series

Rescuing Rayne (FREE!)
Rescuing Aimee (novella)

Rescuing Emily
Rescuing Harley
Marrying Emily (novella)
Rescuing Kassie
Rescuing Bryn
Rescuing Casey
Rescuing Sadie (novella)
Rescuing Wendy
Rescuing Mary
Rescuing Macie (Novella)

Badge of Honor: Texas Heroes Series

Justice for Mackenzie (FREE!)
Justice for Mickie
Justice for Corrie
Justice for Laine (novella)
Shelter for Elizabeth
Justice for Boone
Shelter for Adeline
Shelter for Sophie
Justice for Erin
Justice for Milena
Shelter for Blythe
Justice for Hope
Shelter for Quinn
Shelter for Koren
Shelter for Penelope

SEAL of Protection Series

Protecting Caroline (FREE!)
Protecting Alabama
Protecting Fiona
Marrying Caroline (novella)
Protecting Summer

BOOKS BY SUSAN STOKER

Protecting Cheyenne
Protecting Jessyka
Protecting Julie (novella)
Protecting Melody
Protecting the Future
Protecting Kiera (novella)
Protecting Alabama's Kids (novella)
Protecting Dakota

New York Times, USA Today and *Wall Street Journal* Bestselling Author Susan Stoker has a heart as big as the state of Tennessee where she lives, but this all American girl has also spent the last fourteen years living in Missouri, California, Colorado, Indiana, and Texas. She's married to a retired Army man who now gets to follow *her* around the country.

www.stokeraces.com
www.AcesPress.com
susan@stokeraces.com

Made in United States
Cleveland, OH
17 April 2025